PATRÓN

G·K
Hall
&Co.

Also by Tom W. Blackburn
in Large Print:

Yanqui
Ranchero
El Segundo

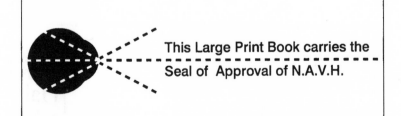

This Large Print Book carries the
Seal of Approval of N.A.V.H.

PATRÓN

TOM W. BLACKBURN

G.K. Hall & Co. • Thorndike, Maine

G.K. Hall Large Print Paperback Series.

The text of this Large Print edition is unabridged.
Other aspects of the book may vary from the original edition.

Set in 16 pt. Plantin by Anne Bradeen.

Printed in the United States on permanent paper.

Library of Congress Cataloging-in-Publication Data

Blackburn, Thomas Wakefield.
   Patrón / Tom W. Blackburn.
     p. cm.
     ISBN 0-7838-9112-1 (lg. print : sc : alk. paper)
    1. Large type books.   I. Title.

PS3552.L3422 P38 2000
813′.54—dc21
                                       00-031960

LT-W

PATRÓN

CHAPTER 1

A small knoll lifted ahead, commanding the gentle slope of the westward prairie into the cottonwood meanders of the Arkansas bottoms. Stanton reined up on the summit of this and looked back. The cattle were coming along steadily, moving as placidly as the river.

There were thirty-five hundred head, each wearing the crown brand of the Stanton ranch. A fortune on the hoof and less than two hundred miles left to go, all downhill now to the river towns. Stanton hooked a knee over the horn of his saddle and watched the herd contentedly. His eyes idly searched for Tito.

Roberto — Robertito — Tito to the house women before he could sit up — had from infancy grown strong in the tall Stanton mold with much of his mother's sultry fire and more than a trace of her fine Spanish features. But 'Mana

Stanton had not wanted her firstborn to accompany the drive.

"Spence, be reasonable!" she had protested. "Might as well take Quelí or the baby. You're in too big a hurry to make Tito into a man. Not yet quite fourteen and already you and Jaime and Amelio and Hugo and the rest of the crew have him believing that he can do anything the rest of you can and just as well."

"Damn near can," Stanton had grinned. "He'll make a hand for sure by the time we get back."

"It's too dangerous," 'Mana had insisted. "The first drive, hundreds and hundreds of miles through the good God only knows what kinds of deserts and difficulties. Maybe months on the trail . . ."

"That's exactly why I want him along. To be a part of something that's never been done before — or even tried. He has a right to look back on something more than the ranch yard and a soft bed and a full belly."

'Mana was not convinced.

"He'll have you to look back on. All his life. The things you'll do when you set your mind. That's enough remembering for any grown man, Spencer Stanton!"

But she had relented as Stanton had known she would when she'd had her say and failed to budge him in his intent.

Tito had been riding right point at the head of

the herd all morning with Hugo, the renegade black who had chosen at great personal risk to turn against the band of ruffians with which he rode and stand with the Corona at a time of grave danger for them all.

That had been long ago, when men of his color were rare in the Territory and there had been problems because of that, but Hugo's loyalty had been unswerving. It was still. Now he was as New Mexican as any of them.

Stanton knew nothing of the powerful black man's past. Nothing had been volunteered and he had never asked. He had no need. It was enough to know that Hugo was one of the wisest men he had ever known, stable and devoted and misleadingly gentle in spite of his enormous physical strength. The Corona was his life.

Hugo was now riding alone. His great Roman head was as always defiantly hatless under the blazing sun. Stanton's eyes drifted back in search over the moving cattle. He finally spotted his son.

Tito was rocking on the seat of the chuck wagon with old Amelio. His pony was on lead at the tailgate. It seemed a fair bet he had scrounged a leftover piece of this morning's pie from the old man. They had been shameless conspirators since the boy could first toddle about.

A flicker of motion drew Stanton's attention back to Hugo. He was signaling. Stanton reined swiftly about. A party of horsemen had ridden up out of thick bottom timber tracing the banks of the Arkansas. They were making straight toward him, riding briskly and tightly bunched as men will when they are on a common cause.

Stanton stabbed his free boot back into its stirrup and rode out at an easy lope to meet them. Behind him he heard other horses kick up as the nearest of his crew came up along the herd to back him if need be.

These men from the bottoms were a hard-used lot. They were poorly clothed for the most part and soil-stained. They were lank and angular with thin faces and hard, suspicious eyes. Their boots were low-heeled and run over, their stock and tack sorry, and few sat a decent seat as they rode.

Stanton knew them at once for what they were. Farmers. Impoverished and disillusioned men who had abandoned worn-out Eastern stone-fields and blackjack Southern hill patches in hope of a new start on virgin soil.

He was surprised. He knew such a tide was inevitable but he had not expected to encounter their kind already so far west of the Missouri. This was grass country and should remain so. Plows would not prosper here. He eyed them curiously, reading their purposefulness and respecting it.

At a dozen yards he reined up, hand upraised in signal to his crewmen coming up behind him. They fanned out to either side and stopped abreast of him. The farmers pulled up in similar array, twenty-five or thirty reasonably well-armed men, outnumbering his crew by twice in both men and weapons.

One among them, better groomed and seemingly more prosperous, appeared to be their spokesman. He looked out over the now halted cattle.

"Passel of beef," he said to Stanton. "You bossing this outfit?"

"I own it," Stanton said quietly.

The man's eyes widened slightly in some show of respect, but the hard flatness of his tone did not change.

"Big man," he conceded. "But you've got 'em pointed in the wrong direction, mister."

"I don't think so," Stanton corrected. "The Missouri's still yonder where it used to be, isn't it? St. Joe — Leavenworth — Westport?"

The man nodded.

"And a lot of people betwixt there and here that are calling this side of the river their country now. People like us. They say half a million acres of sod's been turned already this season and a quarter million more put to pasture."

"So?"

"We been warned you was coming. Six or eight big drives like this, we hear. You're the first to show and we're turning you back right here."

"Why?"

"This land's clean and our stock's healthy. We aim to keep it that way. We don't want your tick-raddled, stinking Texas beeves within a hundred miles of us and, mister, we ain't going to have 'em!"

There was a restless stir of grim assent among the farmers. Stanton suddenly understood. These were mostly unlettered men with the hearsay fears of their kind. In many ways they knew as little of husbandry as they did geography. And they instinctively exaggerated any menace of which they had no personal knowledge or factual understanding.

In some brushy lowland areas in the extreme south of Texas, stock ticks had been found to be carriers of the highly infectious and dreaded splenetic or blackwater fever, usually fatal to their hosts. In recent years occasional epidemics had killed many wild brush cattle in the thickets along both sides of the Rio Grande. There was no known cure or control except quarantine.

Stanton recalled that he and Jaime Henry, his foreman, had felt obliged to kill several of the wild longhorns he had brought in from Texas to bolster his original tiny herd of Eastern beef. They had burned the carcasses as an additional precaution. Further infestations did not reappear. Texas ticks could not survive the high country of the ranch. It seemed unlikely they could survive this far north either. The concern was useless. But if these determined men, new to this country, needed reassurance, they were entitled to it.

"These cattle have never been in Texas or anywhere near tick country," he said. "They came from my ranch in New Mexico. The Corona. Over against the mountains."

"New Mexico!" The spokesman for the farmers snorted incredulously. "Hell, beef cattle can't be drove that far. Nigh a thousand miles by the Santa Fe Trail."

"Nearer seven hundred by the time we reach the Missouri."

"Bullshit! Can't be done. Them are Texas longhorns. How many'd you lose to runny-gut and blackwater on the way north?"

"None," Stanton answered with thinning patience. "I haven't seen a tick in a dozen years, infested or not. My stock's as clean as your own barn-lot milkers and I'm taking them through to the Missouri."

The spokesman glanced at his companions. A sullen mutter ran through them again, but there was no shift of weapons or other overt move. The leader turned back to Stanton.

"There'll be a better time and place. You've been warned. There's a lot more than just us out here and you're still a long way from the river."

The farmer stopped. His eyes ran along the line of swarthy faces flanking Stanton. They came at last to rest upon Hugo. He had been their real target in the first place. The man's lips skinned back from yellow teeth.

"Something else we don't cotton to in this piece of country these days. That's a black-assed, runaway nigger, riding a fine horse and doing a white man's job for pay. That black boy's going to wind hisself up hangin' from a cottonwood tree."

"You've got Hugo scared right out of his skin," Stanton said evenly. "Me, too."

"Your damned greasers ain't no better off. They could be mistook real easy. You think on that, mister!"

"I think I've had enough of your goddamned mouth," Stanton snapped. "Get the hell out of our way or do something about it."

"Big man like you ain't no more trouble than the next," the farmer yelled angrily. "Just takes him longer to hit the ground is all."

He jerked his reins, kicked clumsily at the barrel of his horse with wide-forking, spurless heels, and loped off the way he had come. His companions streamed after him without looking back.

There was silence among the Corona crew for a moment. Then came Tito's voice, calmly stating a considered and mature judgment.

"Now there is one real, ring-tailed, hairy-eared, yellow-bellied son of a bitch!"

Stanton turned to his son. The boy sat there indignantly, unselfconscious among the Corona men. Stanton nodded sober assent.

"That he is, son." Lifting his reins he spoke to the crew. "Move them out. Toward the river. If we can find some fordable shallows we'll try to cross before dark."

The Arkansas was still deep and deceptively

swift-running with melt from the distant and no longer visible mountains. Stanton felt a curious unease on these flatlands. He thought the crew shared it. There was a marked decrease in the banter and horseplay usual earlier in their forty-day trek.

After their years in the high country — a lifetime for most of them — they were aliens in a strange land. Their instincts were not as infallible here, their perceptions not as swift and acute. Vague unfamiliarities flashed many small warnings which usually proved meaningless. But each required a constant state of heightened awareness which was sobering and left little time for camaraderie.

They found three promising shallow sand hooks below meanders of the river. In each case, testing the crossing, Stanton rode unexpectedly off into a deep channel before he was a third of the way across. Failing to find a suitable ford, they bunched the herd at sunset and camped again on the near bank.

Stanton was growing impatient. His restlessness had been compounded by the confrontation with the farmers. Soon the Arkansas would make its big bend off to the south toward its distant confluence with the Mississippi. They would have to cross before then.

His hope was that once out of the broad Arkansas valley, they could follow smaller streams to the north on toward the Missouri with less likelihood of encountering further fringes of settlement. He did not like these ragtag earthbreakers and wished to avoid them if he could. In numbers they could stop anything, even a drive of this size. They were not a challenge to be deliberately provoked.

Thus preoccupied, Stanton nevertheless found a moment after supper to be with Tito apart from the others as his son rolled into his blankets. He squatted on his heels beside him.

"A man cuts his mark in his own way," he said quietly. "Some in one style, some another. I don't admire one that tries to do it with his mouth. Or boy either. Understand?"

"Yes, sir. What I said about that man back yonder."

"How you said it anyway. Rough words are for rough times. When there's no other way to get out what's inside of you. Save them. There may come a time when you'll need them and wish you had more."

"Yes, sir."

"You're doing a man's job. Doing it fine. Let it go at that. The whiskers can come later."

Stanton rose and crossed to his war bag. He returned to his son.

"It's time, I think," he said. "Catch . . ."

He dropped a small, heavy bundle onto the boy's blanket-covered belly. Tito grunted protestingly at the unexpected impact. His eyes widened as he discovered the bundle was a Mexican holster in which nested a brass-mounted Navy Colt with a shortened and rebalanced barrel and grips which had been shaved down to fit a juvenile hand better.

"Good night, son."

Stanton turned away. The look in Tito's eyes was enough. Words often did not pass easily between them in moments like this. Stanton knew he would catch holy hell from his wife when 'Mana learned of this gift, secretly ordered from Santa Fe. But he also knew he was right. It *was* time.

They had faced armed and hostile men today. As they had been warned, the Corona herd was yet a long way from the river towns.

CHAPTER 2

Hugo and Raúl Archuleta were hunkered by the dying fire. Two sober and silent men. Benny and Ramón, Raúl's grown sons, were out with the bedded cattle on first nighthawk shift. Next to old Amelio, the Archuleta family were the first occupants of the little adobe village that had grown up below the big Corona house. There were younger boys growing up who also would ride for the crown-shaped brand of the Stanton ranch.

Raúl was mentor and peacemaker among the *vaqueros*. It was not one to which he had been assigned. He had merely assumed it as the crew grew. Over the years Stanton had many occasions to be grateful for his sound good sense and calm, firm judgment.

Stanton knew a matter of moment was afoot. Amelio, supper cleanup finished, was asleep on the hammock-like tarp tight-stretched as a carryall from the running gear under the wagon. The rest of the crew had turned into their soogans a little distance away.

Approaching the fire, Stanton squatted on his heels, back to the night, facing Hugo and Raúl. He picked up a twig and rolled it between his fingers, studying their dark faces in the flickering light. They waited him out.

"All right," he finally invited. "Let's have it."

Raúl Archuleta looked to the black man.

"Those plow-noses, Spence," Hugo said. "You were wrong when they stopped us back there. They did scare the hell out of me. Raúl, too."

"You tell me," Stanton snorted. "Hell'd freeze over before either one of you would spook at anything on two legs."

"Oh, it ain't like that," the black man protested quickly. "Not scared that way. Not of them. It's how they think."

"Most of them don't."

"How they feel, then. How they can work theirselves up when they bunch together. They're all right with their own kind, maybe, but it sure don't go no further."

"Come on now. You don't believe they actually mean that hogwash about a cottonwood tree?"

"I do," Hugo agreed earnestly. "About Raúl's people, too. Bullheads like them have got two notions they won't stand no trifling with: their own reading of the Holy Writ and the sacred color of their own hides. A nigger's a nigger, slave or free. A greaser's a greaser. They'll see to it that such keep their place, by God, or get learned a lesson they won't forget."

Stanton shook his head.

"Big on talk, short on do."

"Sure," Hugo agreed. "One at a time they're yellow-bellies. But when enough of them get together . . . you ever see a backwoods prayer meeting when it really catches afire? They get theirselves so het up they'd hang Old Nick if they could catch him. When they can't, they'll turn on any poor bastard long as he's different than them.

"That's when they're dangerous. And it looks like we're going to be up to our ass in them from here on to the river."

Stanton scowled. It was this kind of talk that was dangerous. Borrowing trouble. That they didn't need. The cattle were enough.

"Forget them," he said sharply. "I'll guarantee you this: nobody's going to lay hand to a man of my crew."

"Lordy, Spence," Hugo protested, "that ain't what we're worried about. Not us. Christ, no. It's you."

"Me?"

"They'll keep on believing you're a Texan, which ain't much better'n a Papist or a greaser or a nigger by their lights. They'll keep on believing your beef carries Texas fever. Or you aim to graze off their crops or steal their market or whatever else riles 'em. But mostly they'll keep pumping theirselves up that you got a runaway buck nigger slave and a foreign greaser crew that you treat like they was equals.

"That they can get their teeth into. The lot of them. Anybody else that wants to join in. They'll claim it ain't legal and it ain't decent and it ain't Christian. Sooner or later they'll hold you to account."

"Forget it, I told you," Stanton snapped irritably. "They won't stop us. I'll guarantee that, too."

Hugo shook his head stubbornly.

"They won't have to stop *us*. Not the cattle. Not me or the *vaqueros*. Just you. One man and the job's done. You got to walk easy, Spence. And watch sharp."

"*Es verdad, Patrón*," Raúl seconded gravely.

Annoyed at their persistence, Stanton surged impatiently to his feet, lurching a little to retain his balance after the cramp of squatting.

The sudden, unanticipated movement saved him.

A bullet whistled through the space he had occupied an instant before. It struck the ground somewhere beyond the fire and whanged viciously off into the night. From out in the moonless dark on the other side of the camp came the hard, flat report of a heavily charged rifle.

Stanton scooped up the nearly full water bucket set by for night usage and doused the fire, instantly killing all light. He heard the whisper of turned-back soogans as his other men peeled from their beds, coming quickly toward him.

Out on the bedground a few restless steers lumbered uneasily to their feet. One of the nighthawks' voices came softly, singsonging reassuringly as he rode among them.

A figure brushed tentatively against Stanton and came to rest there, motionless. He dropped a hand and discovered Tito beside him. The Navy Colt, too new to have yet been charged, was clutched in his fist. The boy let out a pent breath at Stanton's touch. All else was silence.

The moment held interminably. The shot had been fired upriver, the way they had come. The stir and occasional lowing of the cattle had covered any sound of approach. The incoming tracks of the animals would mask any trace of retreat. The bushwhacker was already gone as effectively as if he had never been there.

A horse soft-footed in from the bedground, ridden as carefully as a man could manage in the blackness. Saddle leather creaked as its rider pulled up, sensing the presence of the others as they did his.

"What was that shot?" Benny Archuleta's voice asked softly, taut with concern.

"We don't know," Stanton answered him. "No harm done. Get back to the herd, just in case."

The horse moved again and was gone. Hugo spoke within a yard of Stanton.

"See? I could say me and Raúl told you the old

22

cow would eat the grindstone."

"Not if you don't want to lose some teeth," Stanton growled.

Tito started to say something but checked abruptly. Some distance out into the darkness on the downriver side of the camp a man hailed loudly.

"You, there — the camp! In the camp, there — I want to come in. Show me a light."

Stanton touched Tito's shoulder.

"Get a candle lantern from Amelio and light it on the tailgate of the chuck wagon. But keep out of the shine."

The boy moved silently away. Stanton heard the murmur as he spoke to Amelio. A bin clattered softly as it was opened. A match rasped on the far side of the wagon and the lantern was set on the tailgate, driving the night back. Tito and Amelio remained hidden.

The lantern revealed the Corona crew as tightly and efficiently gathered about Stanton as if they had grouped defensively there in the full light of day. He nodded approvingly and made a little circling motion with his hand.

The *vaqueros* began falling back in individual directions, each man to a position about the perimeter of the camp, where they disappeared one by one at the limit of light. There remained only the doused fire, the empty beds, and the lantern flickering on the tailgate of the chuck wagon.

The silence returned, to be broken presently by the soft sounds of a guarded but not stealthy approach. A man appeared from the direction of the downriver hail. He was afoot and was leading an unsweated horse. He carried a heavy, brassbound rifle in his free hand and wore two belted pistols.

He was not a particularly big man, a good three or four fingers shorter than Stanton, but he was unusually well framed and muscled. His features were square and strong, with an agreeable, open cast. His clothing was of good quality and he wore it well, moving with an easy, unconscious grace. Stanton saw that his stout but expensive boots had riding heels.

Leaving his horse at the edge of light, he came on in slowly, looking about with a prudent man's care. Passing the overturned bucket and the steam of the freshly wetted fire, he bent to set the bucket upright so as to avoid scuffing dirt into it.

In the full light at the wagon, he laid his rifle on the tailgate beside the lantern and opened the saddle jacket he wore to extract the pistols from his belt. He put these down beside the long gun and stepped away, leaning his back against a wagon wheel to wait. His eyes ran the encircling darkness without uncertainty or impatience.

Satisfied the stranger was alone, Stanton stepped back into view. At once the rest of the Corona crew reappeared, moving in from all sides. The man against the wagon wheel remained motionless.

"I heard that shot," he said as Stanton came up to him. "Bushwhacker?"

24

"Doubt it was a friend."

"Not likely. Anyone hit?"

Stanton shook his head.

"Who were they after?"

"Me."

The man glanced at the muddy ash of the quenched fire.

"Had you silhouetted, eh? Any idea who?"

"Not yet," Stanton answered.

He stepped to the lowered tailgate of the wagon and picked up the rifle lying there. He saw it was charged and capped. There had been time for that since the shot. There had been time between the shot and the hail for a good horseman to circle from one side of the camp to the other, too. He dropped the butt of the rifle to the ground to examine its muzzle.

It was a big-caliber bore. By the sound of the shot the weapon firing it had been heavily charged. Under such circumstances — a heavy charge behind a heavy ball — there was usually considerable smoke leakage as the ball left the muzzle, depositing telltale evidence of recent firing.

Stanton pressed the heel of his hand down on the muzzle of the rifle and rotated it. When he held his hand up for all to see, there was a black ring of powder smudge impressed on his hand.

Understanding the significance, the Corona hands moved in tighter, anger in their eyes. Stanton found Tito beside him once more. The new, yet uncharged pistol was again gripped tightly in his hand. Stanton glanced at it in reproof. Tito thrust it sheepishly back into his waistband.

Unperturbed by the hostile faces, the man leaning against the wagon wheel smiled.

He turned to Stanton. "You know your guns, mister." He nodded at the rifle. "I shot a buck muley at the Crossing just before sunset. Table was getting poor and scarce where I've been staying. No chance to clean her since."

Stanton put the rifle back on the tailgate and slowly wiped the powder soot from his palm.

"You don't believe me," the man said.

"No."

The man turned to Tito.

"Think you can find another candle, son? Light it and run it out a hundred paces or so, away from your stock. Then stand clear."

Tito glanced at Stanton, who nodded permission. Amelio found him a candle and lighted it. Sheltering the flame with his hand, Tito trotted off into the night. When the flame had shrunk to a mere pinpoint of light, the man against the wagon wheel whistled. Tito put the candle down. A moment later he whistled back in signal he was clear.

Stanton handed the man the big rifle. He stepped out a little way from the wagon and stood with his back to the distant, flickering mark, the weapon held loosely across his body. Suddenly he wheeled, the rifle leaping to his shoulder. It fired and the pinpoint of light

26

winked out. Methodically, he began recharging the weapon.

Tito came running back breathlessly, clutching the candle stub. The wick was gone but the tallow had not been touched. Stanton picked up the belt guns lying on the tailgate and handed them back to their owner.

"All right," he said. "You wouldn't have missed. Accidentally anyway. I'm Spencer Stanton. The Corona Grant. New Mexico."

"Yes. New Mexico. So I heard. John Kinchloe, Stanton."

"You have business with me?"

"Worth discussing. To mutual benefit."

"Go ahead, Kinchloe. Discuss."

"You want to get this herd to the river towns. I need gainful employment."

"As a hand?"

"Hardly," Kinchloe said amiably. "You're peddling beef. I'm peddling what you might call influence. I've got a lot of it. Near as much as you have cattle. We can trade a little of each and both profit."

"How little?"

"I'm not greedy. One head in twenty when I've got you through to the settlements and found you the highest bidder in Leavenworth. You'll get the best price there for this big a herd. I guarantee you that. And no more of what you ran into this afternoon and tonight."

"Seems fair. If you can deliver."

"I can and will. You've been looking for a ford.

Only one on this whole strip of river's about four miles down. The Crossing. Where them sodbusters come from. That bushwhacker, too, though we'd play hell to prove it now. They're some riled. I got my work cut out with them tonight. But I can handle 'em. Break camp and come on downriver in the morning. I'll meet you somewhere along."

As though this completed the transaction, Kinchloe strode across to his horse, booted his rifle, and swung up. But he rode back into the lantern light.

"Just one thing, Stanton," he said. "You sure those aren't Texas cattle out there?"

"I said so once today. That's enough."

"No ticks? They're too touchy on that. No deal if there's one infested steer."

"No ticks."

Kinchloe shook his head.

"You sure are something," he marveled. "You and your boys. New Mexican cattle. On the hoof. This far east. That's going to take some convincing."

He looked down at Tito.

"We get a chance to get acquainted, boy, I'll show you some things about that brand-new gun of yours. See you remind me."

He nodded at the candle lantern on the tailgate of the wagon.

"I'd douse that light and keep a watch posted till daylight. If that bushwhacker's still out there, he might make another try before I can get my licks in with them. They're almighty cussed and stubborn that way."

Kinchloe kicked up his horse and jogged into the night. Hugo let out a long breath.

"The sneaking bastards!" he growled. "He sure must have a passel of influence. I'd feel a sight better if I knew what kind."

"We'll find out," Stanton said shortly. "Kill the lantern and the rest of you turn in. I'll take first watch."

CHAPTER 3

The balance of the night passed uneventfully.
They watered the herd and soon after sunup got
it strung out of the bottoms into the open and
onto the better footing of flanking prairie sod.
From here they could see blue smoke down the
river and shortly they came to the first of the
fields.

Each was enclosed and separated from its
neighbors only by its own outermost furrow.
Tito had never seen turned earth in such quantity. Some of the patches were beginning to green
with crop.

Hugo, riding beside him, suddenly held up his
hand.

"Listen . . ."

Tito heard the barking of dogs.

"Settlement," the black man said. "Friend
Kinchloe had better keep his word. Soon."

Tito nodded and surreptitiously touched the grips of the new gun holstered at his belt. He had charged and capped it at the breakfast fire and the unaccustomed feeling of its weight was reassuring.

He was not sure how much of a friend the man who had come out of the night would prove to be. He knew his father was not either. Or Hugo. Or any of the rest of the crew. Most of them, because they best understood Spanish, had been obliged to work out the details of John Kinchloe's proposition at secondhand among themselves. Their uncertainty was obvious in the way they rode. There was none of the usual easy slouch in the saddle against the warm monotony of the long day ahead.

Each man sat erect and alert and they kept the cattle bunched up much tighter than usual. If a stray bolted it was hazed back silently without the normal string of exasperated but good-natured yells. Spencer Stanton was a few rods out in advance, setting their pace and picking the way without looking back.

Across the river a track rutted by wagons came down across the prairie from the northeast and disappeared into bottom timber where the smoke hung. Presently, on their own side, they reached a similar track coming up from the south toward the same riverbank destination. John Kinchloe was waiting for them.

He was dressed and mounted and armed as he had been the night before. The only additions were a war bag and bedroll on the cantle of his saddle. Tito left Hugo and spurred forward curiously to be present when Spencer Stanton and Kinchloe met. Kinchloe waved toward the smoke over the bottoms as he pulled up.

"Pawnee Crossing," he said. "About the newest town in Kansas, I reckon. Damn fools built right on the ford. We'll have to go up their street. May rile 'em some. I argued with 'em half the night, but there's still a few diehards left."

"How you going to avoid trouble then?" Stanton asked, frowning.

"Guts," Kinchloe answered matter-of-factly. "How else in a tight? What got you this far, isn't it? Take your steers down this track and straight on through to the river. I'll be at your elbow. Just you and your men sit tight. Anything I start I can finish. Can't say the same if some of you start it for me. Don't crowd my luck."

"Don't crowd mine."

"Seems fair."

Kinchloe kicked up and rode back along the herd to the chuck wagon. Spencer Stanton started forward and the drive resumed. Tito felt he might be an unwanted distraction to his father out here in the lead. He uncertainly dropped back half the distance to Hugo and Benny Archuleta, riding points.

Kinchloe edged in through dust and the plodding steers to the chuck wagon. He leaned from saddle and passed Amelio his war bag and bedroll. The old man tossed them back under the wagon tilt with those of the rest of the crew.

Kinchloe worked himself out of the press and rode back up along the side of the drive, eyeing the animals he passed. He overtook the point riders and came on to slow beside Tito.

"First-rate beef. Don't see its likes here. Or as big a drive. How many head you run on your range to produce it?"

Tito knew the folly of stating figures in the hearing of curious men.

"Enough now to make a drive like this every season from here on," he answered.

Kinchloe chuckled.

"Close-mouthed. You're being raised right, boy. That new gun. Let's have a look. Toss it here."

Jaime Henry, *segundo* on the Corona and now in charge in their absence, and his father and Heggie Duncan had each spent many hours with Tito, teaching him the handling of firearms, their nature and care.

From a fair rest or even at unhurried offhand in good light, he could nail a mark almost as surely as this man himself had last night. Long gun or pistol. But a firearm was not a toy to be tossed carelessly about.

Nevertheless, he was immensely proud of his father's gift and welcomed this man's interest. He angled over to hand the gun to him. Kinchloe immediately reined away to keep the same distance between them.

"Toss it, I said. Don't worry. I won't drop it."

Tito glanced guiltily about. Up ahead his father was studying the lay before them as they followed the wagon tracks in toward Pawnee Crossing. Behind him Hugo was working his side of the point. Both were engrossed.

He reined again toward Kinchloe but the man pulled away. Tito reluctantly drew the pistol, uneasy with the knowledge that it was in firing condition. He palmed it carefully and swung it in an easy toss toward Kinchloe. As he did so his pony stumbled a little, unbalancing him in his saddle and destroying his aim.

The toss was short and low. The gleaming new weapon seemed certain to pass below the other rider's booted heel and into the dirt beneath his horse. However, in a movement almost too swift to follow, Kinchloe leaned down in a sweeping reach and caught the gun. As he straightened, Tito saw that the grips were solidly set in his hand, his trigger finger was in the guard, and the hammer was eared back for instant firing.

Kinchloe rode over to him and returned the weapon.

"Try it again," he invited.

This time Tito made a fair toss, straight to him. Kinchloe twisted in his saddle and leaned sharply forward. Reaching his left hand behind him with the speed of a striking snake, he caught the spinning weapon at the small of his back. Tito saw that as before the grips landed solidly in his palm, his finger was in the guard, and the hammer was back.

Kinchloe eased back to him, let down the hammer, and handed him the gun.

"I'm not showing off, boy," he said. "Except to teach you something. Think on it a little. It's enough for most men to know where their gun is, on their hip as usual. It's enough for them to find it there fast without missing their grip. They think there will always be time enough for that. Maybe there will be — for meek and peaceful men, if their gun's in the right place when they need it. But it's a chance that shouldn't be taken.

"One mistake, one miss, one fumble is all it takes to get a good man killed. You'll learn that soon enough if you haven't already."

"I've learned a mite," Tito ventured.

Kinchloe smiled. A friendly, almost comradely smile.

"Wouldn't surprise me," he agreed. "With men like your pa and some of these others to teach you."

Tito thought this might call for a demonstration. He slid the pistol back into its holster, then suddenly drew it again with a swiftly striking hand. He laid the weapon across his thigh with a soft slap. The hammer was back and the muzzle rock-steady.

Kinchloe reached up and pushed the brim of his hat back a little.

"Not bad," he said. "You keep on working it from the holster. Keep on honing that down as fine and fast as you can. But start working on getting at it other ways, too. Fast and sure. In your blankets at night. When you're washing up and it's laid aside. Or your belt's hanging from your saddle horn while you're kicking the wind from a blow-belly horse so you can cinch up tight.

"Toss and catch, reach and grab. Every which way you can think of. Till you can get either hand on that gun wherever it is, grips tight to palm, at full cock and finger on the trigger. Even if you're both upside down in midair and traveling fast in opposite directions.

"Like a bad horse fall or you're wing-shot from saddle or you've lost your footing on a rotten slope. Such things happen. There's no use slapping a holster that's already empty. Understand?"

Tito nodded soberly.

"Yes, sir."

"Friends call me Kinch."

"All right. Kinch."

Tito spun the gun back into its holster the way Jaime, more flamboyant in such things than his father, had taught him. Kinchloe tugged the brim of his hat back down and kicked up to overtake Spencer Stanton. Tito followed, hoping he would be allowed to remain with them.

Stanton made no comment when they joined him. The shallow ruts he was following bent down into the bottoms toward the river. Unfenced fields closed in on either side. The roadway between them narrowed. Tito saw that there was bound to be some trampling of the flanking turned earth as the herd passed. Cattle could not be held to such limited space.

His father looked back with the same concern. Shacks and soddies of the settlement appeared ahead where the track reached the bank of the river. Dogs came running out, yapping excited challenge. But before they had covered half the distance they silenced and reversed in slinking retreat, awed and intimidated by the river of beef plodding toward them. Tails tucked, they disappeared among the sorry shanties.

The smoke of breakfast fires was rising from dooryard pits and makeshift chimneys, but there was no sign of inhabitants. There was no sign of the men who had stopped the drive out on the prairie.

Tito saw his father frown sharply as he looked again at the stream of Corona steers cutting the edges of plowed fields to trampled dust behind them. Kinchloe also saw the look.

"No help for it," he said. "They've plowed right to the water's edge. On purpose. So there's no other way to reach the ford. But they've got no right to keep you from it."

"They may have another notion," Stanton said.

"Likely," Kinchloe agreed. "A few anyway. Like I said. A bind comes on, mind you leave them to me."

Stanton looked back again.

"We're playing hell with the edges of their

fields. I don't like that. Unless we pay."

"With what?"

"Money. Reasonable damages."

Kinchloe shrugged.

"If you say. What's a few tromped furrows amount to anyway? It's your money. But be damned if I would."

Stanton made no response. They rode on in silence. The cattle came on steadily behind them. Silence hung over the settlement as well. It seemed deserted — or malevolently in wait.

Then as Stanton and Kinchloe and Tito were among the first makeshift dwellings with Hugo and Benny at point of the herd no more than a few yards behind, the door of a soddy was dragged open. Three men came out. They were the spokesman of the group that had confronted the Corona crew as the drive came in toward the river and two younger men of similar cast.

Each carried a goose gun, big-caliber, loose-shot smoothbores capable of shooting an acre out of the sky on the wing and the belly out of a man at close range. They stalked out into the middle of the track and planted themselves there.

Other doors opened and others of the farmers stepped out, unarmed but with weapons doubtless at hand within their doorframes. If there were women and children, they remained unseen. All eyes were on the three in the street.

"That's just about far enough, Texas," the man who had been spokesman before called to

Stanton. "You and the boy. You don't listen worth a damn and you picked the wrong man for a friend."

Stanton pulled up and Tito reined closer to him. Kinchloe rode on a few paces until a gesture of the spokesman's smoothbore stopped him.

"That's far enough for you, too, Kinchloe."

"Oh, God damn it, McAusland," Kinchloe said wearily. "Quit bowing your back. We settled this last night. Majority's against you."

"Majority ain't always right," McAusland answered. "Too milk-livered when the meat's on the fire. Me an' my sons'll stand it alone if need be. Even against you."

Kinchloe leaned heavily forward on the horn of his saddle.

"I've got a deal with Mr. Stanton. It says his beef goes through."

"Another thing," Spencer Stanton added sharply. "One of you took a shot at me in our camp last night. Who was it?"

"How the hell would I know?"

"And if you did you wouldn't tell me."

"Damn right," the farmer agreed.

Stanton shifted irritably in his seat, but Tito saw he was making a strong effort to accommodate these men.

"Let it go," he said. "He missed. That's what counts. Let's get at this reasonably." Stanton glanced at Kinchloe. "First off, I'll trade you a steer — pick of the lot — for a fresh carcass of game. We've been living too high and need a change."

"Game!" the farmer snorted. "We ain't even seen a buck rabbit since we started turnin' sod, and I told you once we don't want your damn tick-crawling beef."

"Be nice, McAusland," Kinchloe admonished. "Mr. Stanton's trying. He'll even pay you for the furrows we tromped."

"Hell, what's a few hills of crop?" McAusland snapped impatiently. "A boy can replant 'em in half a day. That ain't it. We told the man and he didn't listen. We told you, Kinchloe. You may be the law west of the river. Reckon we got to take that on your say-so till it's proved different. But you'll not put your will on us on our own land for any Texican foreigner. Turn those cattle back or you've rode your last mile. You got three seconds to make up your minds, so help me God!"

McAusland and the two younger men flanking him started to swing the muzzles of their big guns up. Kinchloe's eyes flicked to Tito and his father. Tito saw the sudden, hot, arrogant gleam in them. It was almost as though the Stantons were being told to watch this. Then Kinchloe was facing the three men blocking the track again, and one of his guns was in his hand. Only one. It was enough.

Tito would never have believed a weapon could fire so swiftly. Familiar as he was with guns it seemed utterly impossible. Three incredible, evenly spaced shots in a single drum roll of sound. McAusland's goose gun fired, but he was already falling. Its buckshot charge tore a crater in the ruts, almost at his feet.

One of his sons dropped his unfired weapon and took two steps toward a young woman who screamed from a doorway. His knees buckled with the last surge of his heart and he sprawled heavily. His brother dropped soundlessly in his tracks.

Kinchloe reined to the nearest shanty and gestured the shocked men before it away, putting the building at his back. He raised his voice to the other farmers.

"God going to help any of the rest of you?" he demanded.

None of the men on the street moved. The young woman who had screamed had run out to the fallen man who had started toward her. She dropped to her knees, sobbing quietly beside his body. Kinchloe rocked the gun in his hand.

"Drag them out of our way," he ordered.

Hesitantly, unarmed and uneasy, keeping their faces turned from Kinchloe in aversion, men moved to the bodies, lifted them, and carried them into the soddy from which the woman had burst. An older woman appeared, went defiantly out to the younger, and led her back into the soddy.

Kinchloe turned in arrogance and called to Spencer Stanton.

"All right, Mr. Stanton, move them through."

Tito saw the outrage and anger in his father's

41

eyes and the tight, white set of his jaw, but there was deadly tension here, a few moments of suspended animation which had to be taken advantage of before the inevitable explosion of reaction. Wordlessly, Stanton set his horse in motion. Tito moved with him. The cattle followed. As they rode past Kinchloe he was calmly recharging the fired chambers in the cylinder of his gun.

CHAPTER 4

Fortunately the ford was a good one, wide and
shallow, with a hard bottom and not too strong a
current. The cattle took to it without protest and
the silent riders crossed dry-booted.

The caulked bed of the chuck wagon tended to
float. Raúl Archuleta put a *reata* to the endgate
and lagged back with a little tension on to keep
the wagon from swinging with the current.
Amelio took it across easily, contents unwetted.

Some of the people of the settlement — most
by all appearances — lined the riverbank,
watching the crossing as though all life had come
to a halt except the streaming herd. If there were
arms among them, no attempt was made to use
them. Nevertheless Stanton noted that Kinchloe
trailed warily well behind the drag riders and the
last of the cattle. He was not sure which was the
cause and which the effect.

There were some low bluffs on the far side of the river. Stanton followed the wagon track for half a mile until it had climbed these. Then he veered directly into the northeast across the gently undulating sea of buffalo grass which stretched away interminably in this direction. The cattle, knowing, long travelers that they now were, strung out placidly behind him as though this day was the same as any other on the trail. Pawnee Crossing and the river fell away.

Tito rode tight at Stanton's knee. He glanced occasionally at the boy. A lot of time had flashed past Tito's eyes this morning in a few moments. Time as measured in the making of a man. It had left its mark. Stanton regretted that, along with the event itself, but neither could be undone.

Tito was silent, pale and dark-eyed. Once when he thought Stanton was not looking, he drew his gun and stared at it. Lips tightening, he thrust it back into its holster. Stanton knew the boy wanted to talk, but it would come out in good time. There was no point in hurrying it. And he had his own thoughts with which to deal.

John Kinchloe trotted leisurely up along the herd. He passed close to several Corona hands working the side he rode. Glancing back, Stanton noted that each rider found some task or interest as an excuse to avoid Kinchloe as the man approached. If Kinchloe was aware of the evasions he gave no sign. Presently he drew alongside Stanton, relaxed and unconcerned.

"Think I can keep my side of our bargain now?" he asked.

"Influence, you said," Stanton answered stonily.

"Most powerful there is."

"A fast gun."

"It pays."

"They didn't have a chance."

"Neither would we — me and you and the boy, at least — if they'd got those blunderbusses up."

"Goddamn it, Kinchloe, you've painted us with your brush. I don't like that. I don't like it one damned bit!"

"Christ almighty, Stanton," Kinchloe protested with a first show of exasperation, "you been out in your mountains too long. You let those fields fool you. And their mealymouthed farmer talk. It's dog eat dog in this part of the country these days. Why do you think those thieving rednecks built and planted right on top of the only ford in a hundred miles?"

"Free land."

"Not fit for farming and you know it."

"The bottoms are."

"Oh, hell, for a few seasons maybe," Kinchloe agreed impatiently. "Till the timber's all gone and the river floods 'em out. But that ain't it. They thought you were Texan because Texans is what they been waiting for."

"Natural enough mistake, I reckon. They had some right to get their backs up over Texas fever."

"That pack? Oh, bullshit! Look, grass has been poorly down in the brasada the last few seasons. A lot of hard-pressed Texas bush outfits have been talking about trying some drives north. Word's out on the river that some are already on the way. That's what brought the McAuslands and the rest clean out here. Me, too, far as that goes.

"Get it straight, Stanton. They don't give a damn about Texas ticks or the crops and shanties, either one. They wouldn't have let you turn back even if you'd agreed to. They set themselves up a cattle trap to get first crack at those Texas beeves."

"Baited it funny."

"You showed up bigger than they expected. Little much for them to handle. Most weren't sure what to do about that. So they had a big powwow last night when you wouldn't crack and that bushwhacker missed. McAusland was stubborn. He thought he'd force it and make up their minds for them this morning. That's a lot of cattle back there. A lot of gold on the hoof. Worth the risk."

"You'd have done the same?"

"In his shoes? Hell, yes, if I thought I could," Kinchloe agreed. "But the odds were a little long for one man."

"I believe you would at that," Stanton admitted. "You said you killed a deer just before dark last night. For table meat."

"Right."

"On the edge of a settlement that hasn't even seen a rabbit since plowing started."

"Ever see a farmer with an eye for game or worth a damn as a hunter?"

"McAusland claimed there wasn't a haunch of fresh meat in the Crossing."

Kinchloe shrugged.

"Then one of us lied, didn't he?"

"I'll find out, Kinchloe. Sooner or later."

"Man's got a right to the truth. If he can lay hand to it."

They rode in silence for a few rods. Stanton studied Kinchloe. He was a hard man to read. His easy confidence seemed genuine, his unruffled good nature honest enough. But both were in diametric opposition to the lethal skill and calm unconcern for the suddenly dead that he had demonstrated at Pawnee Crossing. At length Stanton spoke again.

"McAusland called you the law west of the river. On what basis?"

"This. More influence."

Kinchloe reached into a shirt pocket and tossed Stanton a shiny object. It was the badge of a United States marshal.

"Genuine?" Stanton asked.

"Solid silver."

"Damn it, don't play words with me! You know what I mean. Where'd you get it?"

"Fellow on a riverboat. He got to a place where he didn't have much more use for it. Kind of handy in a tight. Specially out here. Sort of a passport."

Stanton weighed the badge in his hand and then tossed it back to Kinchloe. He restored it to his pocket.

"I mind me a draw up ahead directly," Kinchloe said. "Think I'll mosey out and try to flush you up that venison carcass you tried to trade for at the Crossing." He looked at Tito. "Maybe the boy'd like to come along."

Tito hesitated, saying nothing.

"Isn't like it is in your mountains, son," Kinchloe added. "Out there I'd guess game keeps high, pretty much to the open, where it can see danger coming a good ways. Opposite out here on the prairie. Here it mostly stays low in cutbanks and draws to keep off the skyline and out of sight from any distance at all. Takes some doing, but it's a different kind of hunting if you're interested."

Tito made up his mind and nodded. Stanton saw that his son didn't have his rifle boot on his saddle and passed him his own weapon. Tito took the rifle, cradling it across his thighs, and rode off ahead with John Kinchloe.

Stanton continued alone, ordering his impressions and his reaction to them, until the two disappeared over a gentle undulation of the prairie. Then, satisfied with his conclusions, he dropped back until Hugo came alongside with the first of the cattle.

"That was the damnedest thing I ever seen, Spence," the black man said with some awe. "Real sonofabitching sidewinder, ain't he?"

48

Stanton nodded wordlessly.

"Damned if I thought those plow-pushers would try to crowd us this soon or in the way they set out to," Hugo continued.

"Had to," Stanton said. "We forced it on them."

"Kinchloe did," Hugo corrected with a touch of admiration. "But almighty chancy. If he hadn't gotten them three with the scatterguns, you'd both been dead and the rest would have jumped what was left of us. Fat chance to have turned the herd and got the hell out of there with a man still up in saddle. We're sure beholden to that gun of his."

"Kinchloe says they never intended to turn us back," Stanton said quietly, "that they didn't give a damn about Texas fever and aimed to grab the beef. He claims they deliberately set up that settlement at the ford as a cattle trap. We happened to come along instead of one of some Texas drives they're expecting."

Hugo frowned thoughtfully, weighing this.

"It could be, Spence," he said slowly.

"It could," Stanton agreed. "Or it could be Kinchloe wanted the herd for himself."

"One man?" Hugo protested. "Then why'd he throw in with us instead of them?"

"These steers aren't worth a cent more at Pawnee Crossing than they were on the Corona. Only at market on the Missouri. And they've got to be moved a long way yet. Why not join us and let us do the moving — for him?"

"Lordy, lordy," Hugo said softly. "The bastard — if you're right. That's where the big stick'll be. At the river."

"Or close enough to it he can hire help he won't have to take on shares. Nobody there's ever heard of the Corona — yet. Nobody'll give a damn where this beef came from or who owns it. Only who's got it when it gets to the pens."

"Hell, toll him back here," the black man said eagerly. "Now. We can easy find out if that's it. There ought to be enough of us to get that much out of him. In a hurry."

Stanton shook his head.

"I said could be, Hugo, not is. We'll give him his head and see. If he aims to use us, we'll use him. He got us across the Arkansas. There's more settlements ahead; Lord knows what other troubles. This is a big herd. He keeps his side of our bargain and gets us through, we'll keep ours."

Hugo shrugged, disappointed.

"I'll pass word along to the boys."

"Only you," Stanton said sharply. "Just in case. The *vaqueros* don't know this country, these people. They could make mistakes. Wouldn't do to let a man like Kinchloe even suspect we had any doubts. Understand?"

"*Sí, Patrón,*" Hugo agreed resignedly. "But some days you're a mighty hard man to work for."

Dropping behind Hugo, Stanton rode briefly

with others of his crew. A word of assurance here, of commendation there. He knew the imprint of the killings at Pawnee Crossing was strong on most of them. They read omens from such events. They were a religious people. They held their own lives of little enough account if duty required. But the death of others was the will of God. It unnerved them to see a man usurp that power. To a man they greatly feared John Kinchloe.

Stanton sought to assuage that fear in each as best he could. It was a primal emotion and gave those who were feared too great an advantage. Insofar as was possible he wanted to deny that advantage to Kinchloe. So he spoke well of the man and the manner in which he had handled the confrontation at the ford of the Arkansas.

The *vaqueros* listened, but if they believed Stanton could not tell. As long as he had been among them he was an alien and did not know them that well. Nor would he ever. That was for Tito when his time came. Tito was of the land, born upon it, and of his mother. He was one of them. He would be always.

In due time he came alongside the chuck wagon and stepped from stirrup to the seat beside old Amelio. After Jaime Henry, Amelio had been the first hand on the Corona. Crippled in a horse fall so he could no longer ride, early on he had become houseman, cook, and 'Mana Stanton's devoted slave, later mentor and guardian to Tito from the cradle on.

51

Badly handicapped when separated from the wagon that was his domain on the drive, the old man was nevertheless in many ways the most able and dependable hand on the Corona crew.

"Many days have passed," he would sometimes say without vanity. "I have learned my lessons well."

Certainly he had a wisdom and calm confidence which never failed to startle Stanton. He was nothing less than direct in all things. Now as Stanton settled himself on the wagon seat beside him, the old man spoke quietly.

"You tend to your children, I see. So we do not fear."

Amused at the shrewdness, Stanton nodded.

"You wish to speak of those *cabrónes* who died back there awhile ago and of the man who killed them," Amelio continued. "Please to save the breath, *señor*. I have no interest in them. Three are already dead and I do not think the other will live long."

Stanton noted that the old man did not speak in the easy mixed polyglot which had gradually come into use on the Corona in recent years but in the formal old New Mexican Spanish which yet persisted in the mountains where there was little Yankee influence. By this he understood the matter at hand was a serious one and he waited patiently.

"Since he is your son I could not come to you," Amelio went on. "But since you come to me, *Patrón*, I wish to speak of Robertito."

"I listen," Stanton invited agreeably.

"I do not like the gun. The *señora* would not approve."

"You know mothers. Time passes faster than she wants to believe. She'll get used to it."

"I do not worry for her. Roberto is a good boy, but he is not yet a man. You have given him a power but no judgment of when to use it. One is dangerous without the other. The young are not wise. Surely you remember."

Stanton remembered and smiled: a night a year younger than Tito now was which he had spent in the crowded common cell of the old Richmond jail while his father and their most influential friends searched the city for him. His obdurate refusal afterward to admit what he had done or where he had been.

A brawl arrogantly self-provoked in a seamen's tavern on a Virginia waterfront in which his scalp had been split by a stone ale mug and he had broken the knuckles of both hands. The satisfaction that he had walked out upon his own two feet when others could not. His first faltering and unsuccessful adventure with a serving girl in the stable loft at the plantation home of a family friend.

A formal duel on the banks of the James, complete to seconds no older than he and his opponent. The chagrin that neither of the old flintlock pistolets he had sneaked from his father's library wall could be made to fire. The sheepish handshake with his enemy which had

53

won him a friend.

All men had such memories. They were twisted into the thread of life. In time they became an integral part of the fabric and glossed with a vanity they too often did not deserve. But they warmed the heart in recollection. Without them a man was less a man.

He put his hand reassuringly on Amelio's knee.

"I will teach him," he said. "Not to worry, old friend."

The *vaquero* shook his head gravely.

"No, not the gun, *Patrón*. He has found one who knows it better. I do not trust that man he is with."

"Kinchloe?" Stanton protested. "Come on, Amelio, give the devil his due. He got us across the Arkansas. He'll get us to the Missouri. That's his bargain. He'll keep it. He's a good man. As good as they come in his way, I'd guess. We may need him."

"God willing, that may be true," the old man said grudgingly. "Just the same, *con su permiso*, I will watch him."

"You do that," Stanton agreed.

He stepped across into his saddle again, aware of a feeling of reassurance in that simple promise.

Benny Archuleta came up from the drag to point out a party of horsemen overtaking them on a parallel course two or three miles to the south. They were riding at the steady, unhurried pace of men with a long distance to travel. At that distance Stanton could make out little else about them.

A few minutes later they saw Tito's and Kinchloe's unsaddled and hobbled horses ahead, fore-hopping from one clump of thick bunch-grass to the next, contentedly grazing. Their saddles were on the ground nearby, but their riders were not in sight. Signaling Hugo and Raúl Archuleta to keep the drive moving, Stanton rode across to the horses.

Immediately beyond them a brushy, spring-watered little draw opened up. Hanging head down from the lip of a cutbank at its bottom to bleed out was the skinned and gutted carcass of a fat white-tailed mule deer. John Kinchloe was sprawled on the grass near it.

Fifty or sixty feet away, his back to Kinchloe so that he could not presense any movement Kinchloe might make, Tito stood with slightly bent knees, arms hanging loosely at his sides, but with an aura of tautness about him. Both were momentarily unaware of Stanton's presence above them. Kinchloe picked up a clod and suddenly pitched it out, high, so that it landed to Tito's left, slightly behind him.

Tito spun instantly toward it as it struck the earth. Because of the angle it was necessarily an awkward turn but Tito made it with speed and grace without shifting balance, his gun leaping to his hand to line steadily at the point of impact.

Stanton was impressed. He didn't think he could have done as well himself.

"Too tight," Kinchloe called to the boy. "Don't anticipate or you may guess wrong. Let your ears tell your hand to move, not your brain. Takes too long to translate thought to action. Ease up. Hang loose."

Tito holstered his weapon and turned away again. Kinchloe waited a moment, then flung another clod. Some perversity prodded Stanton. He drew his own gun and fired, shattering the clod in midair. Kinchloe twisted in surprise, one of his guns automatically in his hand as he moved. But it was Tito who awed Stanton. He spun like the curling tip of a whip, loose now as he had been ordered, his instantly redrawn gun sighted instinctively.

With a physical jolt of shock Stanton saw that the weapon was at full cock. Tito's face whitened and he closed his eyes as he returned the gun to its holster. As the boy's eyes reopened, Stanton realized that for a fraction of a second he had been very close to serious injury or even death at the hands of his son. It was an unnerving experience and he regretted his own folly.

Tito said nothing as he rode down to them. There was censure in Kinchloe's expression, but he indicated the deer carcass.

"Tito got him," he said. "A running brush shot from a standing horse at better than a hundred yards. Right under the shoulder. Dropped in his tracks. You teach your young'uns good, Stanton."

"So do you, it seems," Stanton answered a little unsteadily. "Fetch the meat and saddle up or we'll have to eat dust."

Tito and Kinchloe slung the carcass between them and followed Stanton back to their horses. They slipped the hobbles and saddled swiftly. Kinchloe heaved the meat up behind his saddle and they rode after the drive.

The drift of air was toward them, and they crossed behind the cattle to the far side to avoid the dust they raised. When they came into the clear there, Kinchloe saw the horsemen who had earlier overtaken the drive now shrinking into the distance ahead. He pulled up and squinted after them.

"What you think?" Stanton asked. "Sure kept clear of us."

"From the Crossing," Kinchloe said. "I know that paint pony."

"More trouble down the line?"

Kinchloe shrugged.

"It's the nature of the critter. Like I said before, you got a lot of beef. A lot of gold on the hoof."

He spoke to his horse and rode in among the plodding steers to take the deer carcass to the chuck wagon. Stanton and Tito resumed toward the head of the drive. Whatever their thoughts, neither spoke.

CHAPTER 5

The country continued to green as the drive descended the long, imperceptible slant of the plains toward the broad valley of the Missouri. The horses of the cavvy, in spite of occasional hard riding, grew sleek and rank-spirited. More than one *vaquero* was piled before breakfast, just for the hell of it, and had to take his hoorawing.

The steers continued to pick up weight on the richer forage. Stanton had hoped that this would prove to be true. It had been a large part of his gamble. Every extra pound on the hoof was additional profit in the pocket.

The practicality of moving New Mexican beef to the river was established. Competition from the poorer longhorn strains reported to have started moving up out of Texas was no threat. Later, perhaps, if they began appearing in quantity or the railroads built to the Missouri and across it, reaching on out into the plains and shortening the routes from Texas to railhead markets. But not now.

The rivers were still the highways. Down the Missouri to St. Louis by flatboat, up the Mississippi to Cairo, then the Ohio into the heart of the East or onto the nearest rails, wherever the highest price prevailed. Western-bred beef, cheap, plentiful, and better table fare than any farm lot could produce. A new direction in the flow of trade and the Corona would be at the forefront. It made good thinking.

Twice smoke on the horizon betrayed other settlements. In each case Stanton ordered a detour farther to the north to avoid them. It added to time and distance and John Kinchloe protested.

"You'll be coming through again next year and the year after," he argued. "Texans behind you if they had it right at Pawnee Crossing. More settlements all the time. Too many to dodge, directly. Better to bull through now. Like we did back yonder. Mark your road so's they'll get used to it. Shove a cob up their ass and learn 'em right the first time. Keep on giving ground now and they'll hassle every herd that follows."

Stanton had no illusions about the obstinacy of a hardscrabble people claiming new land. For some obdurate reason their sense of possession was more jealous over what they had taken without leave than over what they had legally claimed or inherited from their fathers and their fathers before them. And their defensiveness became more determined the more they were contested.

He knew that Kinchloe's argument was probably valid enough. Most prudent men respected an aggressor who came head on and no nonsense if only because they feared him. But in the interests of his own men as well as his stock, he was anxious to avoid further confrontations such as that at the crossing of the Arkansas if at all possible. Word of that now preceded them. There was bound to be reaction. Larger and more determined forces might be gathering. So they made the detours.

However, a line of low chalk hills began to push up out of the prairie parallel to their course. They were gaunt, scrub-sided, and bald-knobbed, forming a considerable barrier. The chalk formation progressively hardened into coarse limestone and became more sheer on its lee face, presenting a line of cliffs which presently swung south across their way, forcing them to search out a pass through it.

This proved to be the wide, shallow, serpentine canyon of a summer-dry watercourse wet with occasional spring-fed pools barely adequate to water the herd. Bottom grass was correspondingly curtailed. A day and a half into this, too far for any practical attempt to double back out, they encountered a stretch once heavily timbered which had been ruthlessly cut out.

What remained was a sickening litter of high

stumps and top-hamper which had been lopped off and left to rot. On down the canyon a few miles a tall plume of smoke presaging a considerable settlement again hung in the sky, and no detour was possible here. At the next water, Stanton called a halt.

Penned in by the sidewalls of the canyon, the cattle would need little attention. He ordered Tito and Amelio to remain with the herd and rode on with the rest of the crew, hoping to make as impressive an appearance as possible. It seemed the best way to bargain if necessary for uncontested passage.

Because of the meanders of the canyon, the saddle distance to the source of the smoke was greater than had at first seemed. The ruts of the wagons that had logged out the bottoms grew deeper the farther they followed them. It was well into dusk when the first sounds of settlement reached them — ragged, sporadic gunfire.

Stanton recognized the flat, heavy jolt of handguns interspersed with the sharper, higher crack of rifles. The pattern of the sounds and the comparative frequency of the two types of reports conveyed a clear enough message to a man who knew guns. One faction, probably forted up in some shelter where they could afford reloading time between each shot, was using the longer range and more accurate rifles against a mounted attack limited to the multicharge revolvers which were the only practical weapon in the saddle.

"Somebody's sure trying to shoot the hell out of somebody," Kinchloe said, reining in close.

Hugo moved in to Stanton's other knee.

"Whatever it is, it's nothing for us to be riding into, Spence. It just don't sound very welcome at all."

"I don't know," Stanton answered thoughtfully. "If we pick the right side it may be just what we need. Let's mosey on in a ways and take a look."

He turned in his saddle and looked back at the crew, then spoke to Kinchloe.

"You and Hugo take the Archuletas and move over as tight under the right wall as you can. I'll take the rest over under the left. If we chance it to mix in, we'd best come from two sides. Doubles the surprise."

"If we don't get one," Kinchloe growled. "Light's going fast. How are we to know?"

"If I give you a whistle, go in fast. Head for the handguns but stay clear of those rifles."

"And if you can't make it out or decide not to chance it?"

"We'll cross over to you and pound leather back to the herd."

Kinchloe shrugged.

"Just one thing, Stanton," he said. "We go in, we'll be shooting for meat?"

"They will be if they can. Don't give them the chance."

Kinchloe nodded satisfaction and tilted his head at Hugo. The black man dropped back and returned with Raúl Archuleta and his two sons. Kinchloe took the lead and they rode toward the right canyon wall, fading into the shadows thickening at its base. Stanton veered to the left and the rest of the crew followed him toward the opposing cliff face there, spurring up as he did.

They rode swiftly and as silently as possible. Watching for occasional glimpses of the other party, Stanton saw that Kinchloe, Hugo, and the Archuletas were doing the same thing, pacing themselves so that they remained abreast of him. The going was good and he kicked up a little more, knowing the gun sound ahead would cover their approach, and the men behind the guns were likely too busy to note if they were occasionally revealed.

In less than a mile the canyon turned abruptly and widened out. In the center of this open space was the source of the smoke toward which they had been riding. Stanton pulled up in astonishment. Glancing across he saw that Kinchloe had also halted momentarily, and for the same reason.

Near a great rick of logs cut to length and split for fuel were three haystack-like kilns. They were shaped of limestone quarried from the canyon walls and Stanton had no idea of their use but the deep cherry glow from their vents in the increasing darkness attested to their efficiency. Two unhitched logging wagons stood near the huge woodpile. Back of this was a stout corral in which a number of horses, both draft and saddle, were milling nervously.

Beyond the glowing kilns was a scatter of half a dozen buildings along both sides of a short, broad street. They, too, were laid up of uniformly cut limestone blocks and heavily roofed with sod over closely set logs. Whoever had put them up had meant them to be permanent and perhaps the beginning of something even more ambitious.

The largest structure, its small, high windows yellow with lamplight, appeared to be a warehouse or store of some sort. Four or five saddled horses were tied to another unhitched wagon behind it. Stanton judged their riders were within.

The rest of the buildings seemed to be houses or living quarters. All were dark, but rifles were firing sporadically from two across the street from the larger structure. By the rate of fire, taking into account recharging time, Stanton thought there must be three or four riflemen in each, rotating at apertures or firing ports.

Their targets were low-riding horsemen, flung to the far side of their mounts as they flashed past any area of exposure to defensive rifle fire. With necessarily limited visibility from within the unlighted smaller structures and the increasing darkness without, it was almost impossible for the defenders to line the raiders up in their long-barreled sights.

It was equally impossible to tell with any accuracy how many of them there were. They were riding fast and in random pattern, circling and darting among the other buildings and appearing unexpectedly for a moment by ones and twos from all directions, using their handguns only enough to keep the riflemen pinned where they were and without enough sustained firepower to make an effective sortie.

Nevertheless, Stanton was certain the horsemen were strictly a diversion. It was the old Indian game of a surround to keep defense immobilized. He was convinced that the real purpose of the attack was being carried out by those within the lighted larger building and whose horses were waiting behind it.

He watched a moment longer, making up his mind, then spoke quietly to his *vaqueros.*

"All right, *amigos,* let's break it up. Mind your powder. Any of you gets himself shot up he'll have to answer to me."

Raising two fingers to his teeth he sent a piercing blast echoing across the canyon and jumped his horse into a flat, full run. He had a glimpse of Kinchloe, Hugo, and the Archuletas also in motion under the opposite wall and pulling a little ahead of his own group.

He realized they were trying to build enough lead to circle behind the buildings on their side so as to come in at the far end of the little street. He slowed the pace slightly to let them gain the ground they needed and held straight for the glowing kilns.

The sullen red light from the banked fires within made an effective screen to cover their approach so long as it was between them and their objective. The human eye automatically searches out a light source in the dark and seldom can focus effectively beyond it. Then they were at the kilns and past and the reverse was true, the kiln fires now lighting their way but throwing them into sharp relief.

Even so, they were not seen for a moment longer and were at the head of the street. Kinchloe, Hugo, and the Archuletas appeared simultaneously at the far end, and somewhere in between a man bellowed hoarse alarm. A gun flashed in their direction to punctuate the warning.

The shout could have been misread in the confusion as an expletive of excitement or a roar of anger. The shot was lost among others. A rider burst from between buildings, saw the two converging parties on the street, and tried to turn back. Stanton followed his turn with the muzzle of his pistol, anticipating a little, and fired. The man lost his weapon but remained up and disappeared the way he had come.

Stanton reined hard in the opposite direction, shouldering his men into a between-buildings slot there to avoid running the gauntlet of defending rifles forted up a little farther on. They could not identify themselves as friendly in the uproar of men and horses, nor could the riflemen be expected to separate them from their enemies in this light.

Another rider, coming hell-bent through the

slot in the opposite direction, collided with them there. Reyes Martinez, beside Stanton, quickly lifted a foot from his stirrup and planted its sharp, spurred Mexican heel in the man's belly. He went backward over the crupper and fell beneath the feet of their horses.

They burst into the open at the rear of the buildings. A few rods farther on, Kinchloe and his companions broke from a similar passage to the street. Three startled riders, suddenly finding themselves trapped between two hostile forces they neither anticipated nor understood, milled frantically. Kinchloe rode straight through them, emptying two saddles as he did so. Hugo nailed the third as he fought for control of his horse.

Kinchloe brushed alongside Stanton.

"How many in the big place with the lights?" he shouted.

"Five — six, by the horses out back."

"Better root 'em out before they all hole up there."

"You and Hugo and I," Stanton agreed. "Raúl, take over. Keep 'em moving. Crowd the hell out of them before they can figure out what's happening."

Raúl Archuleta rose in his stirrups, swinging his hat.

"*Venga, compadres,*" he cried. "*Ándale! Para La Corona.*"

The *vaqueros* spurred after him along the backs of the buildings toward the far end of the street to make another sweep. Stanton, Hugo, and Kinchloe, riding abreast for as much show as possible, cut back between buildings toward the fronts opposite. As they reached the street, Stanton saw that the alarm had now become general.

The door of the lighted larger building had been swung inward and gaped widely, spilling a broad shaft of light. Men were darting out, sprinting for the corner and their horses tied in back. Behind them Stanton had a glimpse of the mischief they had been about — a tumble of broken crates and overturned barrels.

A few steps into the street, silhouetted by the yellow-framed doorway, a man with an awesomely stentorian voice was bellowing orders and gesticulating angrily with a stubby, heavy, muzzle-loading carbine he carried in one hand. He was an imposing figure, gaunt, a head taller than his fellows, with a great, full beard and hair hanging below his shoulders, both bleached a startling white.

Doors across opened cautiously, and the defending riflemen who had been holed up there began to emerge guardedly. Two fired at the bearded man with no visible effect, but it was hasty shooting. The heavy carbine appeared to be discharged, for the bearded man made no attempt to use it. The men who had raced for their horses at the rear charged back around the corner flattened in their saddles. One was leading a big, gray riding mule.

At the same moment light struck Hugo and the bearded man saw him.

"A nigger!" he roared. "Get him. The Lord wants his sinning soul."

Fighting his own horse, the man leading the mule came alongside and thrust the reins at the bearded man.

"Leave be, 'Lige," he yelled. "Let's get to hell out of here!"

The rider spurred on after the rest. The bearded man vaulted astride the mule. Too late Stanton saw the man had pulled a huge saddle-pistol from his rig and was leveling it at Hugo. Stanton realized he was blocking Kinchloe, and he tried to turn his horse to a better angle as he lined his own weapon.

The bearded man was before him. He heard the big slug strike his horse. Its head dropped as though pole axed. The front quarters went and it somersaulted, landing atop him with crushing force. Dust was in his mouth and a roaring in his ears. He fell through it into a black and silent void.

CHAPTER 6

Stanton lay helplessly on the flat of his back. Stabbing pain racked every bone and muscle in his body. Even breathing was a wheezing and agonized process he would have willingly avoided if he could.

He opened his eyes. Close-spaced, peeled logs supporting a sod roof were overhead. White-washed stone walls surrounded him. So protected, the little room was cool despite the sun blazing beyond glazed and solidly framed windows.

He lay on a stout bed covered with quilting. A rustic chair sat beside the bed. A hand-planked clothespress stood against one wall. A small, braided rag rug was on the stone floor. There was no other furniture except an iron bracket from which the lamp was missing.

He became aware there was half a bottle of

what was hopefully whiskey on the seat of the chair. Thinking it to be as good an antidote for pain as could likely be had, he tried to reach for it. His whole body cried out in protest at the effort and a wave of blackness submerged him again.

Small hands were upon him when he resurfaced. They were gentle in touch but strong and calloused with labor. They belonged to a face. It was round, rosy with sun and weather and framed by two long, thick braids of gleaming yellow hair. The eyes were a startlingly bright blue, expressive and concerned. The mouth was large, soft, the lips red and full.

The girl was young, perhaps half through her teens, but the bodice of her dress could not conceal the high, firm breasts thrust against it or her skirt the trimness of her waist and the strong mold of her thighs. Stanton did not know about angels but he thought this would do for a model until a better came along.

She was offering something in a bowl to him. He opened his mouth and accepted the spoon she held out. It was a pungent broth. It tasted unpleasantly like a concoction 'Mana had learned from the Utes and which had been a medicinal staple on the Corona since the first brush shelter that had been their honeymoon quarters on the grant.

He had never been able to abide the acrid herbal flavor, however miraculous the medicinal powers 'Mana claimed for the liquid. He could not now. He grimaced and his eyes sought the bottle on the chair.

The girl laughed in quick delight that his senses were sharpening. She put down the bowl, uncorked the bottle, and held it to him so that he could pull from the neck. He took two great swallows. It was surprisingly good whiskey — the best he could remember since he had abandoned Virginia and all things Virginian to head west.

The girl replaced the bottle and ran excitedly from the room. She was back in a moment with a formidable figure of a man. His hair was also yellow and his face as round as hers. The paternal kinship was obvious.

He was of no more than average height but Stanton had never seen more powerful shoulders and chest or a greater belly. It thrust out before him like the staves of a stout barrel. There was no hint of fat. It was as solid and heavily muscled as the rest of his body.

This impressive torso was set upon massive, trunklike legs. They carried it lightly with surprisingly quick and graceful movement.

The impression of enormous physical strength was in strange contrast to the genial affability of the rounded features and the twinkling eyes. The voice was a Wagnerian bass which boomed from the cavernous interior.

"Ach, Gott, Kati," he said to his daughter, as pleased as she was, "you are right. He lives yet."

He picked up the bottle of whiskey and measured its lowered level with an approving eye.

"Jakob Meier, *Herr* Stanton. Please to be the guest of this house. You must be of iron. Never have I seen a man take such a fall. The whole weight of that dead horse on you. It took eight of us and two stout poles to lift it off."

"That I believe," Stanton wheezed. "How badly am I hurt?"

Meier glanced at his daughter and then to the door. Stanton saw that Kinchloe, Tito, and old Amelio were standing there, hats in hand. Thus exposed they had the white, shaded foreheads and ear tips and the bronzed faces, necks, and hands of saddlemen. Even his son, who had his long time astride a horse yet to come, bore these telltale marks of the cattle country.

"Hell, cover up and come on in," he ordered testily, hurting for the air it took to form the words. "This isn't a God damn wake!"

They moved a little into the room uncertainly.

"Bad?" Meier repeated. "A little inconvenience for even you, I think. How many broken ribs I don't know. I'm a mechanic, not a doctor. But none were driven into the lungs. There is no blood in your spit. Another drink?"

Stanton nodded weakly. Kati Meier returned the bottle of whiskey to his lips. He took another swallow and waved the bottle away.

"*Gut*," Meier approved. "*Gut* medicine. Bruised everywhere, I think. In another day you'll look like your nigger boy. Black all over. Later all purple and yellow. You live so you don't die. But there is the leg. Your stirrup foot. A nasty break of the shin. Splintered, out through the flesh. Kati and I put it back as best we could. I carved a splint to fit. To hold it straight, I hope. You won't walk or ride for a spell."

Stanton took this stonily.

"How long?"

"Snow-fly," Meier said cheerfully. "Maybe spring. But not to worry, *Herr* Stanton. You are welcome here after last night."

"Shit!" Stanton breathed softly.

He tried to explore his lower left leg beneath the quilt but could not make the effort in spite of the warming whiskey. He looked at Tito and thought that this was how a man grew old — overnight, with everything riding on him, and by a stupid mischance.

"What the hell was it we rode into?" he asked, not really giving a damn now.

"Politics," Meier said. "Thievery. Little difference here. Not like Pennsylvania, where we come from. There the Amish, the Friends, the Dutch all good friends. Here, not even made a territory yet and they call her bloody Kansas. The slave question. For the votes in Congress when the time comes. That one who shot your horse — the tall one with the white hair — he didn't mean to do that. You rode into his way."

"Not on purpose. I can tell you that."

"Elijah Ames his name is. He calls himself the Missouri Prophet, appointed by the Lord to make this slave territory. Actually an unprincipled ruffian. Many of the same ride with him

74

when they see loot to be had. It was your black man he intended. He hates to see them free. They say he's killed over a hundred by his own hand."

"His bunch sure didn't expect us. What were they after?"

Meier shrugged.

"Horses, stores, money. We have a business here. A small profit in gold put by. Maybe Kati, some of the other women. Such men are like that. But mostly to drive us out, I think. Maybe kill us even. Before the vote comes.

"Many such raids are made out of the Missouri hills these days. Many excuses. But that is always the real reason. Many like us have been made to give up and go back where they came from. Many have died."

"Where's your law?"

"Law, when there's not even any government?" Meier snorted. "But not to talk so much now. These are our troubles, not yours. Your boy wants to see you. And these men. Good men, *Herr* Stanton. All of them. We're beholden."

Meier smiled warmly and left. His daughter went with him. Stanton saw Kinchloe's eyes follow her as she passed. Tito and Amelio came diffidently to the bedside. Tito was taut as a spring, his eyes frightened and dark with the anguish of anxiety.

Even Amelio was childlike in his deep concern. Stanton realized he must offer both some tangible reassurance. Words alone would not be enough for either.

Forcing a smile to cover the agony even slight movement cost him, he sat slowly up in the bed, carefully drew his knees up, and clasped his hands over them.

"You missed a tolerable bit of excitement last night, son," he said.

Tito nodded wordlessly.

"Seems like I had my share and have to pay a mite for it," Stanton continued. "But don't let what the Dutchmen say worry you. Can't expect Pennsylvanians to understand what tough *hombres* we Corona New Mexicans are. We'll be back on the trail again in a few days and no harm done."

Stanton unclasped one hand from his knees, balled it into a fist, and rocked it lightly against the line of Tito's jaw in a gesture familiar to them both. The boy nodded again, closed his eyes, re-opened them, and smiled wanly. His pallor warmed in a flood of relief. Amelio crossed himself in gratitude.

"I'm sure glad, *Patrón,*" Tito said. "I was sure scared when Kinch brought the word and we got down here and first saw you."

Stanton opened his hand and dropped it to Tito's shoulder, gently massaging the strong young muscles there.

"Naturally. First time you ever saw me flat on my back, out like a lamp in the wind. So I've got a few dents and dings. That's all."

"But your leg?"

"Bunged some. Sore as hell. But we'll lead the herd into Leavenworth together, just like we started out. Meantime you can do something for me so it'll be ready when I am. You're good with a punch and awl. Check my rig over to see if I split any leather or cracked the tree. It may take some fixing."

"Sure," Tito agreed eagerly, anxious for something for his hands to do. Waiting was not easy for the young.

Stanton nodded at Amelio. The old man understood.

"*Venga,* Roberto," he said. "We'll get at it now. He has promised. He'll mend fast."

The two left. Kinchloe sauntered over, picked up the whiskey bottle from the chair, sat down, and sampled it.

"Whooee!" he breathed appreciatively. "Roanoke, by god! These folks live good. And we can have anything they've got. They buried five of those bastards this morning. The Prophet raised a little hell with their storehouse but he didn't find their gold. None of them were hurt and neither were any of the *vaqueros.* For strangers we done 'em quite some favor."

"The idea, wasn't it?" Stanton grunted. "Not going to be any problem moving the herd through?"

"Was some. Too damned much volunteer help. Dutchmen underfoot every which way. We brought it down this morning. It's on a meadow a couple miles on. Open country beyond. As far's the beef's concerned, Leavenworth's a hell of a lot closer than it was yesterday."

"I know," Stanton said. "Except for me. Time enough for Leavenworth when we get there, Kinch. What the hell's in those kilns we saw burning last night?"

"Damnedest operation you ever saw," Kinchloe answered with genuine admiration. "Leave it to the Dutch. They'd make a business out of prairie-dog holes."

"What kind of business?"

"Indians call this place Manykill. Before they had horses they'd make a surround afoot four-five times a year and stampede as many buffalo as they figured they'd need over the north rim of the canyon. For god knows how many years. There's a stack of bones out there you wouldn't believe."

"Bones are a business?"

"Sort of dust to dust returneth," Kinchloe agreed. "Meier's got eight–nine families here. Relations. Cousins and the like. Hard-working bastards. They fire those old bones with a little limestone and grind the lot up with some char-coal from the fires. Then they sack it up and freight it to the river for fertilizer."

Stanton had a great respect for ingenuity. He understood Kinchloe's admiration.

"I'll be damned," he said.

"Lot of cotton country down toward New Orleans," Kinchloe continued. "Cotton raises hell with any soil in a few years if it ain't mineralized every so often. They're selling all they can make and Meier's got a dozen more families of relatives on their way out here. Due any day."

"That ought to end his troubles with Missouri raiders."

"So he figures. He'll have thirty-forty able-bodied men then. Hold off an army behind these walls. But he's some worried about feeding 'em. He'd like to buy some beef from you. Enough to tide 'em over until they can knock off for a fall hunt or stock up at the river."

"Whatever they want," Stanton agreed. "Twenty-five dollars a head."

"Kind of steep, ain't it? This ain't Leavenworth."

Stanton was wearying, but he realized that Kinchloe had not yet gotten around to the real subject on his mind.

"I've done better at Sante Fe in small lots and I intend to do better at Leavenworth," he said.

Kinchloe shrugged and picked up the bottle of whiskey. He extended it in wordless invitation. Stanton declined with a gesture. Kinchloe took a small, thoughtful pull and leaned forward earnestly, elbows on knees.

"Look, Stanton, I'm not faulting, but we've kind of got our tail in a crack with you laid up. Ain't nobody else going to buy your beef while it's hung up way out here."

"Let 'em graze on some more weight till I'm ready to move. It's not going to be all that long in spite of what Meier says."

"No way," Kinchloe said flatly. "Grass and water where they are won't hold 'em more'n three days at most."

"You said the country opened up again on yonder. Drift 'em on a little farther when necessary."

Kinchloe shook his head stubbornly.

"That's asking for it. One of the raiders the Dutchmen buried this morning was from Pawnee Crossing. Time that bearded bastard that knocked your horse down and the rest of them get home, every renegade in Missouri will know there's thirty-five hundred head of prime beef out here to be had for the pickings."

"We'll have to chance it," Stanton said with rising impatience. "We've had to before."

"Not at the odds shaping up now. I'm no fool in these things, Stanton. You ought to know that by now. I don't like the cut of this Elijah Ames. He can raise too many men."

"He didn't have enough last night. And fewer this morning."

"That's another thing," Kinchloe said with a puzzled scowl. "The son of a bitch has got some kind of a charmed life or something."

"What do you mean?"

"He was standing out there in the light in the front of the storehouse, yelling orders with every Dutchman who had a load in his rifle banging at him and they never touched him."

"Goes to prove what you said before: farmers

are no marksmen."

"Yeah, but when you went down and I could shoot over you, I got two clean tries at him before his mule got around the corner of the building. He stayed up. That don't happen, mister. It just don't happen."

Stanton tried to shift his weight on the palms of his hands, breathing painfully.

"You spooking? Maybe welshing on our deal?" he asked.

"Hell, no! I'm trying to keep my promise," Kinchloe answered, anger surfacing. He calmed and continued. "Be reasonable, man. There's only one thing to do and you know it. It's no part of the deal but I've got no more choice than you do."

"No, Kinch."

"That beef's got to keep moving, just as fast as we can hustle it, now. I'll leave the boy and Amelio here with you. Somebody else can drive the chuck wagon. I'll deliver the herd to Leavenworth and get you the best price I can for it and I'll kill any bastard who tries to stop me."

"No," Stanton repeated.

"What's more, I'll return your crew to you here before I claim my share of the take," Kinchloe pleaded earnestly. "And no change in the percentage we agreed on. You'll have to trust me for it."

Stanton shook his head, sagging wearily and knowing he was not up to further argument.

"I learned my lessons the hard way, Kinchloe,"

81

he said. "Some men I trust. But none with a woman or money. Graze for three days where they are, you said. In three days we go. All of us."

Kinchloe's eyes hardened. He started to protest further but broke off as though realizing the uselessness of the effort. Stanton could feel the hard pressure of his disapproval and knew it did not have far to go to become defiance. He also knew he could not control Kinchloe now and so would have to think ahead of him in all things until he was back on his feet.

"If you want to be a Goddamned fool . . ." Kinchloe growled.

He hooked up the bottle of whiskey and angrily drained half of its remaining contents.

Kati Meier returned. Kinchloe quickly put the bottle down and gallantly rose to offer her the chair, all trace of anger gone in an instant. Kati refused with a smile and came to the bedside.

"It is for you to lie down," she said to Stanton. "Now you sleep again. Then we will bathe the leg and I will bring you some soup." She saw his wry expression and laughed. "No, good soup this time. Not the medicine. I promise."

Stanton eased back down. She straightened the quilting over him, then picked up the whiskey bottle from the floor and marched out with it. Kinchloe's head followed her passage and he started after her.

"Kinch —" Stanton called, stopping the man in the doorway. "None of that. The girl. We friended them here and they friended us. Keep it that way, you hear?"

Kinchloe looked out the door after Kati then back to Stanton.

"We got no agreement on that," he said. "You're forgetting something. I ain't your nigger or your boy or one of your greasers."

He stepped on out and was gone.

CHAPTER 7

Two men lived in John Kinchloe. One was a man of conscience and pride, of substance and responsibility, with a decent respect for his fellowman, howsoever he found him. The other was hard and brutal, with a high, flaring recklessness and utterly no regard for any living creature but himself.

On occasion the two melded and lived in peace. Those were the tranquil times. Then Kinchloe slept well. The hell came whenever one nature or the other surged to dominance. There was a deep hatred and scorn between the two. Whichever temporarily achieved the upper hand turned savagely upon the other and sought to destroy it, to permanently erase it from his consciousness.

Whenever this happened, Kinchloe was in torment. He was in torment now. He knew his anger at Spencer Stanton was unreasonable. He knew the rancher was not responsible for the situation in which they now found themselves. It was the result of a physical accident which could have happened to any of them. But he also knew he had killed men for no better reason.

Meier's daughter was swinging along the street toward the storehouse, and he thought her back-side would waggle just as enticingly under a man as it did here in the sun. He thought of Stanton's orders concerning her. The arrogant fool.

Patrón. A big word the way his boy and his *vaqueros* used it. Meaningless here under the circumstances. To Jack Kinchloe at any rate.

Wait till Stanton saw that leg of his where the white bone had been sticking through the flesh when they picked him up. Wait till the big-headed bastard tried to do more than just sit up with those stove-in ribs. It had taken sand all right to make a show like that in front of the kid and the old man in there. But that's all it had been — show. And not much at that. Orders, hell!

Kinchloe sauntered across the street. Up toward the bone kilns he could hear axes or splitting mauls ringing at the woodpile and a grating rumble he supposed was the stones of the Dutchmen's mill or whatever kind of a grinder they had rigged. The men all seemed now at work. Likely the women, too, since no others but Meier's girl were visible about.

Tito Stanton and the old Mexican cookie were

squatted beside Stanton's saddle on the shady side of the storehouse. He paused before them briefly. They were soaping out a bad scuff on the crown of the saddlehorn. The rig seemed otherwise undamaged.

"Could have been worse, eh?" he said to the boy.

Tito nodded.

"I was sure afraid it was going to be."

"Yeah. Know what your pa just told me? We're moving on in three days. He knows it's impossible. He always that stubborn?"

"Mostly," Tito agreed with a grin. "When he's got something he aims to get done."

"And does he — does he get it done?"

"Always."

"Some *hombre*," Kinchloe said.

He looked back along the street. It was empty. The rest of the Corona crew was down with the cattle as he had ordered. He went around the corner of the storehouse to the door and followed Kati Meier within.

The debris from the raid had already been straightened up and the big room tidied. The girl was facing him over a big stone crock from which she was paddling snowy-white fresh lard. Bending, her dress gaped and he could see the pendant, creamy swell of her breasts. She looked up as he pushed the door closed behind him, then smiled and straightened with the paddle of lard mounded on a pie tin. Her curiosity was unselfconscious.

"You look for me?"

"Uh-huh," Kinchloe agreed, moving slowly toward her. "And the looking is mighty good, honey. It surely is."

"*Ach,*" she laughed deprecatingly. "It is only that I am Dutch. You do not see so many *frauleinen,* I think."

"Not near enough," Kinchloe said, stopping before her and rocking a little on the balls of his feet. "Not near enough of you either. Not yet. You got a man here?"

Beginning to frown a little in puzzlement, the girl shook her head.

"Why not? Don't you want one?"

She tried to smile again but it was uncertain now.

"I think of it sometimes," she admitted. "But here they are all my uncles and cousins."

Kinchloe started to reach for her but she stepped gracefully past him and took a canister of fine-grain gunpowder from a shelf. She opened it and poured half a cup of its contents over the lard on the pie tin.

"For *Herr* Stanton," she explained as she began to stir the mixture together with the paddle. "A poultice for the leg. There is maybe something else you want me to do for him?"

"No," Kinchloe answered, "for me."

This time she could not elude him. He took the tin from her and set it aside. He caught her by the elbows and pulled her urgently to him, his hands sliding up under her arms. She resisted but he pressed her back against the shelving, pinning her there with his body.

His mouth clamped over her lips. His tongue sought hers. One shoulder of her dress fell and warm flesh was in his palm. His grip tightened insistently. He felt the nipple erect firmly beneath his touch.

Suddenly resistance ran from her. Lips softening, she came against him, helplessly, cheeks wetting with silent tears. Kinchloe drank voraciously of her. Her breath quickened. His own senses began to reel. While he still could, he freed her and stepped back. Lips parted, she covered herself and stared at him with great, rounded eyes.

"When you go back over there, you tell Stanton what I done to you," Kinchloe said raggedly. "Tell it as scary as you want. Tell him I'll do it again directly, till I've had my fill. Tell him to hell with him. Understand? To hell with him!"

Kati Meier nodded dumbly. Kinchloe headed blindly for the door. When he looked back there, she had turned her back and was mechanically tearing strips of bandaging from a bolt of white muslin on a roller. He stepped out into the sun.

Tito Stanton and Amelio had finished their chore with Stanton's saddle. Amelio was hobbling up the street toward Jakob Meier's house. Tito came around the corner of the storehouse and nearly collided with Kinchloe. Now that he'd had his satisfaction two ways at once, Kinchloe was in a better frame of mind, his anger ebbing.

He saw a shadow of himself in the boy and liked him. Young Stanton had a curious inner gift which he himself possessed, a channel of communication between mind and muscle infinitely faster than normal. Under certain stimuli it almost seemed the body thought for itself and so responded with no lag for even reflexes to react.

Other men had died for want of this gift. Kinchloe lived by it. So in time would Tito Stanton. He moved with the light-footed, instantaneous response of a pronghorn. He sat a saddle as few men ever did, automatically anticipating and adjusting to the slightest movement of his horse so that he was as much a part of the animal as its own body.

Already he handled the lightened Navy Colt his father had given him better than any man on the Corona crew, including Spencer Stanton himself. It was a vanity Kinchloe fancied that the boy would handle it better than any man he was ever likely to meet before Jack Kinchloe was finished with him and they came to a separation of their ways.

"Finished?" he asked, indicating Stanton's saddle, now soaped to a shine and racked on an overturned keg against the wall of the building

Tito nodded. Kinchloe drew one of his own guns and spun the cylinder briskly.

"Want to mosey out yonder a way and show me a thing or two?"

"Any time I show you," the boy answered. "But I'd admire to try."

They started off toward the far wall of the canyon, walking abreast. When they were out a way into the open from the street, Kinchloe began to lag imperceptibly back a portion of a stride so as to ease his silhouette from the tail of the boy's eye enough to render it indistinct.

When he thought the placement right, he slapped for his gun. It was a trick which had never failed him but it did now. At the first hint of movement, perhaps even before there was any, Tito whirled toward him. The muzzle of the boy's gun clicked against the buckle of his belt while his own weapon was still rising.

Kinchloe remembered the scene on the back trail when Stanton had come upon them in the draw where they had killed a deer. Stanton had been behind them, unseen, yet the response had been almost as instantaneous. But the boy had had his father's shot to trigger him then.

"How the hell did you do that?" he growled, startled in spite of himself.

"I — I don't know," Tito answered slowly. "Wait. That's it. I *did* know. Somehow. Like on a fractious horse or one strange to you. I knew what you were going to do and when. Just for an instant-like. The way a horse sets his body when the notion strikes him to try something cussed or he's going to change stride or something. You must have given some kind of a signal."

"When you couldn't have more than half-seen me at best? I don't make that kind of a mistake, son. Even in fun."

Tito nodded and shrugged.

"Luck then, I guess."

"Yeah," Kinchloe agreed. "Bad luck for any poor bastard on the wrong end of your gun if you was meaning it for real. But you did two things wrong. You were filling your right hand as you turned but you spun to the left."

Tito twisted a little in experimental recollection and nodded.

"Most humans do when they're startled or want to turn fast for some other reason," Kinchloe said. "Don't ask me why. Maybe because the left's the shoulder we look at the moon over or something. Try it again, now — slow. See how far your right hand has to travel in a left spin before you can line your gun on a target behind you?"

The boy pivoted obediently.

"Now spin to the right," Kinchloe ordered. "See? The same amount of turn but the right hand has a cut less distance to travel. That cut can make a hell of a lot of difference if you're really in a hurry."

"How'd you learn all these things, Kinch?"

"No matter. The important thing's that I never forget 'em. See you don't. Other thing is a gun ain't a knife you got to stab somebody with to make it do its business. It does real good about six feet away and I ain't comfortable any closer.

"You spun right into me as you turned. Jammed your sight into my belt buckle. No need to set a man afire with your muzzle blast just because you aim to kill him. The closer quarters you're in, the more can go wrong. And you're apt to get yourself all splattered up with blood and gut. Maybe yours."

"I'll remember," Tito said. "What else?"

"That'll do for now."

The boy absently holstered his gun and looked curiously at Kinchloe.

"This wasn't what you brought me out here for, was it?" he asked.

"Well, matter of fact, no," Kinchloe admitted. "I don't want to worry you or the boys none, but it's about your pa. He's going to kill himself sure if somebody don't pound some horse sense into his head. He's in no condition to try to go on to the river now, and we can't risk holding the herd out here until he is. Not with half of Missouri on the prowl.

"I tried to talk him into letting me and the crew take the beef on to Leavenworth. We can do your business there as well as he could. With any luck, if he don't try something else foolish, he ought to be in shape to start home in easy stages by the time we get back. But he wouldn't listen to me."

"Why? Doesn't he trust you?"

"I don't know. Reckon I riled him a bit."

"He knows you wouldn't have to come back if

you changed your mind — once the herd was sold and you had the money."

"Then he's got a mighty suspicious nature," Kinchloe protested. "Me go back on my word and cut and run? With that wild-eyed bunch of *vaqueros* riding herd on me? Fat chance. The point is, do you trust me? I think your old man would listen to you and some of the others if you'd kind of talk 'em up to it."

Tito scrubbed the toe of his boot in the dust.

"You sure that's the straight of it, Kinch?"

"As straight as I can tell it, son. My iron's in this fire, too, you know."

"He won't like it," the boy said slowly. "When he wants advice, he asks for it. But if you're right, then he's wrong and he's got to be told. Like you said, for his own good. I suppose it is up to me. I'll ride down and talk to the rest. If he or Amelio asks, tell him I'll be back directly."

Kinchloe dropped an approving hand to Tito's shoulder.

"I'll do that," he said. "You'll make a hand, son."

Young Stanton saddled up behind the Dutchmen's storehouse and rode down Manykill Canyon toward the beef camp at its mouth. Kinchloe went back to the street and pushed the door of the storehouse open. Kati Meier was gone. He supposed she had recrossed the street to attend to the injured man as she had promised.

If so, she'd be having her say about now. Later Stanton would have his. But there wasn't a damned thing he could do about it. Maybe he'd learn to know Jack Kinchloe just that much better. Enough not to meddle in something that was none of his business.

Kinchloe stepped into the storehouse. The nearly finished whiskey bottle the Meier girl had brought across from her father's house stood on a counter. Kinchloe sat on an upended sack of meal and emptied it, sipping slowly to savor the taste, thinking of timing.

It would work out about right if Stanton would listen to reason. If he wouldn't, it would work out anyway. It would have to. That was what Jack Kinchloe had signed on for.

Another day here. Maybe two, if Stanton was stubborn. Meier had said that when the Dutchmen made a shipment their tandem wagon-string took five to six days in good weather to reach the Leavenworth wharf. The Dutch wagons would be heavily laden and on a six-up team. If Stanton's cattle were pushed a little bit, they could be moved at about the same rate.

Say two more days on the river to round up buyers, make the tallies, and collect for the beef. No more than two days back here to Manykill without the impedance of the herd. Twelve days. Two weeks at most. Stanton should be able to travel then. In the chuck wagon, if need be.

In two weeks the Corona would be on its way

back to New Mexico. In two weeks Kinchloe's job would be done and he'd be long gone with profit in his pocket.

The only worry was Elijah Ames. There was no telling how far the Missouri Prophet and his blacklegs had come to make their raid here or how long it would take them to return to their headquarters. There was no way to know whether Ames would recruit a bigger outfit and come back for blood and a try at the Stanton herd or not. Or how long it would take him to do so.

One thing was certain. Once the drive was again on the move, every mile gained lengthened the ride the Missourians would have to make in pursuit. And Ames would not dare to strike too close to the river. Under the circumstances the odds in that respect seemed fair enough. In any event, they had to be accepted.

Prowling, Kinchloe discovered the open case of whiskey and extracted another bottle. He sat back down to get himself drunk slowly. He had nothing better to do and felt he had earned the indulgence.

Beside, the Meier girl might come across from the house again before her people returned from the kilns or Tito Stanton came back from the beef camp. A man could hope.

CHAPTER 8

Amelio sat silently beside the bed. Stanton dozed fitfully. He heard clattering in the kitchen. Presently Kati Meier reappeared with a pie tin of some muddy unguent, some rolls of freshly torn bandaging, and a new bottle of whiskey. She offered Stanton a little of this and sent Amelio to the kitchen for a pan of water she had heating there. Then she went to work on the leg.

It was Stanton's first opportunity to see the injury. With the outer binding stripped away, the ingenious splint Meier had contrived was revealed. It was of two halves, fore and aft, carved and smoothed to fit the contours of the leg. It extended from just under the knee down over the ankle to instep and heel. When in place the two halves fitted neatly together in a hollow whole like a casting mold. The outer binding held it tightly together, giving some measure of rigid support.

With the splint removed, inner bandaging was exposed, stiffened with blood and drainage. It was necessary for Kati to soak this free. She did so as carefully as she could, taking great pains not to move the now unsupported leg as she worked.

There was not as much pain at the outset as Stanton would have supposed, but the hot water bit torn flesh and the room swam giddily a time or two. When the last of the bandaging came away, the wound was shocking. It was a ragged, gaping fissure along the outer edge of the broken shinbone and nearly as long as his hand. It was slowly oozing fluid and in spite of Kati's care Stanton could see it working a little with the involuntary movement of his own breathing.

He realized at once that although Jakob Meier had deliberately exaggerated the length of time he would be laid up, any attempt at an early departure from here might be hazardous in the extreme. He swore softly to himself and at John Kinchloe for good measure.

The man had been right, at least in part. But the devil himself was not going to separate Spencer Stanton from his cattle. He had been too long in accumulating them. They had cost him too much. They represented too much of his life. Only through proper disposal of them could the Corona continue to prosper and grow. Any risk of mismanagement or loss through other hands was too great a chance to take.

With the wound cleansed as thoroughly as she

dared, Kati gently applied her evil-looking unguent. The pain Stanton had anticipated came in full measure then. The salve burned into raw and swollen flesh like living fire. Amelio came swiftly to the bed, obviously fearful Stanton's body would fight the agony and undo Meier's careful work in setting the broken bone.

Stanton waved him away and grimly held himself rigid. Sweat poured from him. Moisture beaded Kati Meier's forehead and upper lip as well.

"It only burns a little while," she said unsteadily. "It is lard and gunpowder. Goose fat and carbolic acid would be better and doesn't hurt so much but we have none. I'm sorry, *Herr* Stanton."

Stanton nodded acceptance. White-faced, she continued the treatment. As she promised, in a little the raging fire mercifully began to subside. The girl covered the wound with a fresh inner bandage. Carefully replacing the halved splint, she rewrapped the outer binding tightly. Stanton was limp but the injured leg felt better, although he knew it was probably mostly out of relief.

"Thanks," he said hoarsely. "You're a good nurse."

Kati wiped the dampness from her face with her apron, smiled, and hurried off toward the kitchen. Stanton turned his head to Amelio.

"Where's Kinchloe?" he asked.

The old man shrugged disinterestedly.

"Yonder someplace," he answered. "With

Roberto, I think. Last I saw at least."

"He pester that girl?"

Amelio's shrug became more elaborate.

"They were in the storehouse for a time. Roberto and I were working on your saddle. I heard no complaint."

"I want to know if he does."

"If I learn of it," Amelio agreed.

Kati Meier returned with a steaming bowl of soup.

"Better get the chuck wagon down to the herd," Stanton told the old man. "There'll be empty bellies down there before dark. Take Kinchloe with you — and Tito, if you can find them."

Amelio nodded and limped out.

Kati sat gingerly on the edge of the bed and offered Stanton a spoon of soup. It was rich and warmed him after the reaction chill of his ordeal. The girl dipped again with earnest attention. He watched the movements of her face and body and suddenly felt old.

It had been a long time since a woman had spoon-fed him. Not since the distant day he had first regained consciousness on Corona grass with the wound of a would-be murderer's bullet in his back and 'Mana had been crouching over him. What had happened in the days after that could not happen here. He meant no disloyalty to 'Mana but he was vaguely sorry for that. Kati Meier was young, but a man was dead who could not feel himself drawn to her.

There was a rattle at the end of the street beyond Stanton's window. The Corona chuck wagon appeared, headed down the canyon with Amelio on the seat. He was alone.

Presently the soup was finished. Kati rose to leave. She straightened the quilting over Stanton and rearranged his pillow. She would also have pulled hemmed sacking across the window against the light but he asked her to leave it be.

She went out, softly closing the door behind her. Stanton did not know if he dozed then but it could only have been a few minutes until Kinchloe appeared afoot beyond the last house at the street's end. He paused there, idling to no apparent purpose, and Stanton watched him curiously.

Almost immediately Kati Meier also appeared. She shot a backward glance toward Manykill village. There seemed no anxiety in her, only a prudent wariness over being seen, but she apparently forgot Stanton's window. She went straight to Kinchloe.

The man's arms engulfed her. She tilted her face up eagerly for his kiss. They pressed against each other in an ardent, moving embrace. Stanton caught a flash of swirling skirt and white thigh before they sank from view in tall grass almost beside the wagon track. He regretted that he had not let the girl draw the curtain across his window after all. He wanted no personal knowledge of what was happening out there in spite of his orders to Amelio. His problems were complex enough as it was.

Stanton slept fitfully the third night at Manykill. His ribs had eased with the commencement of healing, but sometime after the house was asleep his leg commenced a painful throbbing. His mouth dried and he became aware of fever. He also was aware of what it meant. An infection was setting in. Now they would have further ammunition against his determination.

They had come up from the herd a few hours after he had sent Amelio and the chuck wagon down to them the afternoon of the first day. Hugo and Raúl Archuleta and Tito. Two sober and earnest men and a troubled boy. Only Amelio had known Spencer Stanton well enough to accept the futility of argument with the *patrón* of the Corona when his mind was made up. The old man had remained at the beef camp with the younger *vaqueros*.

Kinchloe, grass stains at the knees, joined them when they reached the Dutch village. One of them rode up to the kilns for Jakob Meier. They waited for him before they filed in to where Stanton lay. He had his quiet anger at John Kinchloe, knowing that it was he who had gotten to Tito and through him to Hugo and Raúl.

That had been insubordination, defiance of a direct order. So had his lie with Kati Meier been, no matter what provocation she might have given him, intentional or not. In time he would be obliged to deal with Kinchloe for both.

But he could not fault Hugo and Raúl for their loyal concern or Meier for his offered hospitality and sturdy insistence upon what he believed was common sense. Most of all he could not blame his son for the love he bore him. So he patiently heard them out save for Kinchloe, who had already had his say and wisely remained silent.

However, Stanton's answer was the same, and they left disconsolately, knowing they could do no more.

Now he was not so sure. He tried to keep his lips wet and ignore the heat rising inexorably in him and fretfully waited for the night to pass into first light. Time passed with interminable slowness, measured by the pulse beat throbbing in his injured leg.

Jakob Meier, his round face rosy from a stinging morning scrub, was preparing to change the bandage under the splint and repack it with his daughter's homemade salve when Stanton heard the wagon rattle up outside and he knew his reluctant men had come for him.

"You make the mistake, I tell you," Meier said earnestly as he worked. "The very big mistake, *Herr* Stanton. I wish you would change your mind. That wagon is no featherbed, even for a well man. You will see before you've gone a mile."

"That mile will be one I won't have to travel again," Stanton answered, grateful the Dutchman seemed unaware of the fever gripping him. "Each one will be. Shorter distance each day. I'll do fine."

Meier shrugged. The outer door opened. Hugo and Tito and Raúl Archuleta and his two boys filed in.

"How's it this morning?" Hugo asked anxiously for them all.

"I'm breathing a hell of a lot better anyway," Stanton answered honestly. "That's something."

They nodded and gathered at the foot of the bed to watch Meier's massive hands delicately open the splint and lift the inner bandage. Stanton hitched up a little to see for himself. The bandage came away easily, but with it came a great gout of pus and stray bits of discolored flesh.

Meier's jaw set. He straightened at once and put a palm to Stanton's forehead. He grimaced as he touched the hot skin. He bent again over the leg and probed gently at the skin surrounding the ragged edges of the injury. More pus surfaced, welling up from deep within the wound where the broken bone lay.

"This is no better," Meier said tersely. "And it's going to get a lot worse."

"Then you're not leaving here," Tito cried. "We won't let you, *Padre*. No matter what you say!"

Meier turned to the boy.

"He has to, son. None of you have any choice now, I'm afraid."

"What do you mean?" Stanton asked.

"You're in fever," the Dutchman said. "You know that. It will go higher. In the leg is the trouble. Much infection. Very deep. Near the bone, I think. We have no tools, no medicine, no knowledge what to do with such a sickness here. Soon it will start to stink, I am afraid. A doctor you need. Quick. The closest is at Leavenworth. You must get there as fast as you can."

"Well, at least it doesn't change our plans any, does it?" Stanton grunted. "Get it wrapped up so the boys can load me in the wagon."

Meier wordlessly replaced the stained bandage, but his hands were now trembling in spite of his effort at control. He called for his daughter. She came quickly from elsewhere in the house. Seeing what was wanted she went to work at once, gently replacing the splint and rewrapping the outer bindings. Stanton watched her curiously. She did not even glance at John Kinchloe and he seemed equally disinterested in her presence. When she was finished, she stepped back out of the way.

"Can we carry him out in the featherbed?" Hugo asked Meier.

"*Ach,* take it. Right into the wagon with him. It will softer make the ride."

Stanton started to protest. Meier held up his hand to silence him.

"I insist, *Herr* Stanton," he said firmly. "Extra bags of down we have. Kati can stuff a new one. It keeps her from mischief."

Stanton had his own opinion of that. He gestured Tito to the clothespress.

Tito brought boots, clothing, and guns to the bed. Stanton reached into an inner pocket of his jacket and found what he wanted, a Washington-minted gold double eagle, the principle coinage in which the Santa Fe trade was conducted. He glanced stonily at Kinchloe before speaking to Kati Meier.

"I hope I'm not settling for another's service," he said. "Hold out your hand."

The girl did so and he put the coin in her palm.

"That's yours with my thanks for your care," he continued. "As I told you before, you're a good nurse. Buy yourself something pretty next trip to the river."

The girl's fingers closed over the coin. She curtsied and stepped back. Stanton looked up at Hugo.

"Let's go," he said.

The black man and Raúl Archuleta each took a corner of the bed at the foot. Benny and Ramón Archuleta stationed themselves similarly at the head. At a nod from Hugo all lifted gently in unison and the bed came away from the frame. To get out through the door, it was necessary to fold it partially so that Stanton lay as in a hammock.

The first movement sent a fresh wave of pain through him.

Because of the grub cupboard inside of the tailgate of the chuck wagon, it was necessary to lift him, featherbed and all, in over the front seat. It was awkward and he was a fair burden for four strong men, but they managed smoothly enough. Nevertheless, by the time they had eased the bed down onto the floor of the wagon, Stanton had a pretty fair idea of the kind of hell that lay ahead of him.

If any hope remained that the pain might ease, the last spark died when the wheels started to turn. Stanton gritted his teeth and an involuntary groan escaped him. Tito was over the seat and beside him in an instant. He looked up into the boy's anxious face.

"Aggravation," he granted. "This is sure one hell of a way to travel, isn't it?"

"I wish it was me," Tito whispered.

"Now look here," Stanton protested, "you have some kind of a notion you could stand it better?"

Tito shook his head miserably.

"No, sir. It's just that —"

"Never mind, then. Just no more of that. Time ever comes you get to thinking you're more of a man than your pa, you're going to have to prove it, right then and there. See you keep that in mind."

"Yes, sir."

Stanton tried again to brush a balled fist reassuringly along the line of Tito's jaw, but the familiar gesture no longer seemed worth the effort. Suddenly — not in a normal, gradual submersion — he slept.

When he roused again he could smell the dust. By this he knew they had overtaken the herd which had started ahead of them and were now moving with it. They were on their way. It could be worse. Anything could.

He slept again.

CHAPTER 9

Kinchloe had always relished the feeling of command whenever he could achieve it. Because he enjoyed it, he was an efficient leader. A tough one if need be.

In an hour he had Stanton's *vaqueros* sweating and dust-streaked in the sun. He knew this kind of driving was contrary to their natures and experience, and there was resentment in them because of that. But there was also a new respect for him in their eyes and the herd was moving faster than it had since he had joined the drive. The cattle could afford to melt off a little fat. So could the crew.

Out of respect for its wounded passenger, he had the chuck wagon pulled up ahead of the point where it would be clear of dust and a track pulverized and pocked by the hoofprints of the cattle. Young Stanton was riding on the seat beside Amelio, glancing anxiously every few moments back into the box where his father lay. His horse was at the tailgate.

Kinchloe knew he could not maintain discipline for long with the other crewmen without maintaining it here as well. Besides, it was better for the boy to have other duties to divert his attention. He rode up beside the front hub of the wagon.

"How is he?" he asked.

"He's awfully sick, Kinch," Tito answered worriedly.

"Well, you're not going to make him any better sitting there on your butt. Amelio can keep an eye on him. Hit saddle and get back there on the drag. We got miles to make, damn it."

Tito stared at Kinchloe. The same hard, cold light Kinchloe had seen on occasion in Stanton's eyes flared in the boy's. Then it died. Tito swung out over the wheel, dropped down, and untied his horse. Mounting, he reined hard about and spurred back along the drive.

Kinchloe looked challengingly at Amelio. There was no friendliness in the old man but he nodded approval.

"*Bien*," he said. "But be gentle with him. It is a hard time."

"I know," Kinchloe agreed. "I'm not that much of a bastard. Stanton taking it all right so far?"

Amelio shrugged.

"What can you expect?"

"Yeah." Kinchloe lifted his reins. "I'll work

ahead, find you the smoothest going I can. Fire a shot if I'm needed."

Kinchloe found water for the noon stop. The men were as grateful as the stock but Kinchloe would let none drink their fill in the heat of the day.

It became necessary to get Stanton out of the wagon to relieve himself. The laborious lift over the driving seat was too impractical for the frequency with which it would have to be repeated. Hugo freed the bottom lashing of the wagon tilt on the near side and rolled it far enough up so that the injured man could be helped over the sideboard between the bows. He had to be steadied as he balanced on his good leg in Jakob Meier's too-short but otherwise ridiculously voluminous nightshirt.

Most of the *vaqueros* tried to keep their eyes averted, unwilling to see Spencer Stanton in such straits. Kinchloe wondered exactly what kind of a man the rancher really was that he could exact this much loyalty and respect with no greater effort than was apparent in his relationships with his crew.

The giddy unsteadiness troubled Kinchloe. It seemed likely that as Meier had forewarned, Stanton's fever was still rising. And it was hot under the tilt in the full sun. He went around to the far side and raised the canvas there as well so any breeze could pass freely through.

Hugo climbed into the wagon and rearranged the Dutch featherbed, propping it up with some of the bedrolls so Stanton could sit in a half-reclining position and see out over the sideboards if he wished. When he had been lifted back in and settled upon it, he seemed much more comfortable.

"Fetch me a cigar and let's move," he said in an attempt at jocularity which fooled no one. "Get this wagon back where it belongs, Amelio. I want to see and smell and taste those steers walking themselves to market."

"This wagon stays where I put it," Kinchloe countermanded quietly. "If I'm going to get you to Leavenworth alive."

"I'm kind of set on that myself," Stanton admitted wryly. "Tell me something. You ever been on a drive like this?"

"No. You know that."

"Well, neither have I. Not like this. Neither has anybody else. So I'll give you no argument — long as we keep moving."

Kinchloe gave the string-out order and hung back to see the herd begin to move as the *vaqueros* pressured it. As he rode forward again and passed the wagon, Stanton called to him. He reined over.

"You give orders a hell of a lot better than you take them, don't you?" the injured man asked bluntly.

"You could say that," Kinchloe admitted.

"If I was on my feet I'd have to bust your ass for it."

"Yeah. You'd have to try, I guess." Kinchloe

smiled. "Some ways I'm downright sorry you can't. It'd be some tangle, Stanton."

"That it would," the rancher agreed. "Goddamn it to hell!"

He leaned his head back and closed his eyes.

The next day went as the first, a good twenty miles or more by night stop a full hour after sundown, men and beasts so tired they bedded practically in their tracks. Kinchloe was well satisfied. A third of the distance to Leavenworth was already behind them.

Hugo, self-appointed to the task, again replaced the dressing on Stanton's leg with fresh bandaging provided by Kati Meier. Again there was more pus and the swelling had increased a little so that the two halves of Meier's splint no longer quite came together. Stanton's fever remained high but there seemed to be no spread of the infection and he slept before any of them, resting easily.

In due course, after a last circuit of the bedded herd, Kinchloe also slept. He was awakened in the small hours by an eerie, chilling scream like that of a mating cougar. Amelio fumbled a lantern alight. The sound had come from Spencer Stanton.

He was sitting upright in the wagon, his injured leg drawn up before him, and his fingers were tearing frenziedly at the bindings of his splint. He was deeply flushed. His eyes were wide open but glazed and senseless and he was babbling unintelligibly in the throes of wild de-

112

lirium. In nearly as great a terror, Tito scrambled in to his father, pleading desperately.

Kinchloe roughly hauled the boy from Stanton and thrust him back for others to hold and console as best they could. With Hugo's help he forced Stanton onto his back and pinioned his arms. It took their combined strength and they had to lash blankets over him with tightly pulled ropes to hold him there. He continued his violent attempts to struggle even after they succeeded in completely immobilizing him.

Kinchloe did not know what else could be done. The eyes of the Corona crew told him they did not know either. They waited helplessly in tense and anxious silence. After a little the seizure passed and the stricken man slipped into a shallow-breathing stupor. Kinchloe eased the chest ties then, remembering the injured ribs. He turned to the crew, his mind made up.

"Build up the fire so we have some light," he ordered. "He's got to get to Leavenworth and a doctor right now! Seventy, eighty miles to go. Amelio and Tito can take him."

"Wait a minute, Kinchloe," Hugo protested sharply. "An old man and a boy? They can't even handle him if he goes out of his head again."

"They'll have to," Kinchloe answered harshly. "We may have all hell coming at us from behind, too. With Stanton down we're short one hand already. I'll have to have every able-bodied man with the cattle. Some of you bring in an extra span of good horses with the wagon team.

They're going to have to travel far and fast.

"The rest of you get what we'll need out of the wagon and load any gear we can't carry on our saddles. A blanket apiece and a handful of grub'll do. Get moving. I want them ready to roll at first light."

They scattered. Tito was first, seizing a pair of halters and sprinting into the night toward the horse cavvy.

Kinchloe returned to Stanton and carefully examined him as best he could. The splint was still firmly in place and the violence of his delirium seemed to have caused no further damage there. He did not like the sound of the injured man's breathing and he thought the rate of heartbeat was faster than it should be but he had no real understanding of such matters and could not be sure.

Amelio was hobbling about, setting out saddle grub on the lowered endgate of the chuck wagon for the rest to roll into the blankets Kinchloe had allotted them to sling across their cantles. Kinchloe spoke to him privately.

"Two days, I figure," he said. "You should have clear going with the Dutchmen's wagon tracks to follow. Get the best you can out of your horses, but don't kill 'em, or yourselves either."

"For me, I do not care," the old man answered quietly. "If anything happens to the *patrón* I would die before I could go back to the *rancho* and face the *señora* and the little ones waiting there. I will do my best, *señor.*"

"Drive as long as you have light. Let the boy spell you where the going's good. Keep Stanton as quiet as you can. If he comes to, tell him Jack Kinchloe said he'd deliver these cattle and by God he will."

"*Si*," Amelio nodded, "or it is you who will die. I know *mis amigos* well. The Corona Grant is their home. They will destroy anything that threatens it as they would a rattlesnake on the ground. A good thing to remember, *señor*."

"Christ, doesn't anybody in this damned outfit trust me?" Kinchloe complained.

"Tito, I think," Amelio conceded. "Do not disappoint him."

"We'll be in Leavenworth two days behind you. I hope what you're gaining is enough to save Stanton's life."

"God willing."

The old man resumed his chores.

Tito brought in a fine-looking pair of leaders and they were doubletreed to the end of the wagon tongue ahead of the usual two-up team. The last of the gear was loaded up and saddle rolls laden and tied. Stars were still out but the eastern horizon had begun to loom faintly when Amelio climbed to the seat of the wagon. Kinchloe faced Tito Stanton, hand outstretched.

"Your pa'd be proud of you, boy. You think of that. It'll help."

Tito nodded wordlessly, shook hands, and climbed up beside Amelio. The reins snapped and the wagon rolled.

Tito could not stand the slow, plodding creak of the wagon when the need was for haste. His own body felt the jolts his father's was taking in spite of Amelio's care in keeping to the smoothest ground he could. His impatience was almost unbearable. To ease it he mounted his trailing horse and rode out ahead a quarter of a mile to scout out the best going for the lumbering wagon.

As the sun climbed higher, he doubled back. He saw that the hides of the horses were already beginning to darken with sweat. Amelio was holding them to the best pace they could make. It was useless to hope for more.

Tito stopped the wagon to let the teams blow while he rolled up the sides of the tilt again to let more air beneath the canvas. His father's eyes were closed. They opened and he saw that the injured man was again rational. He smiled encouragingly and lifted the wooden lid of the water barrel lashed to the sideboard to dip a tin cup from it.

He handed this in to Stanton but his father could not manage the cup and Tito had to steady it for him. The injured man drank thirstily and signaled with his eyes for another. Tito refilled the cup and that was also drained. Stanton's fingers plucked protestingly at the rope-bound blankets over him.

"Hot," he said. "This necessary?"

Tito looked at Amelio. The old man nodded soberly.

"To keep you from hurting yourself, *Padre*," Tito said.

"That bad?"

"Last night, for a while. You — you didn't know what you were doing. It was all Kinch and Hugo could do to get you back down."

Stanton tried to smile.

"At least it took two of them." He closed his eyes.

"It'll be all right," Tito assured him as confidently as he could. "We'll have you to a doctor in no time. Just rest easy."

"The cattle. I don't smell their dust."

"Behind, with Kinch and the rest of the crew. They'll catch up with us at Leavenworth."

"How far?"

"Forty-fifty miles," Tito answered, lying a little on the short side. "Tomorrow. Sometime tomorrow."

Stanton nodded. His eyes closed and Tito saw he slept.

Amelio reached back from the seat and felt the *patrón's* brow. He looked at Tito and shook his head gravely but said nothing. Tito understood. That was the hell of it. There were no words and if there were they would be useless. Time was the only thing now. Time.

Tito gulped a drink from the water barrel and swung onto his horse.

"Roll," he told Amelio through tight lips, and he spurred out into the lead again.

CHAPTER 10

Late in the afternoon of the second day after the departure of the chuck wagon, Kinchloe found Amelio's and young Stanton's night camp. He was beginning to fear he had somehow missed it and was delighted they had made it this far before darkness forced them to halt.

They were doing better than he had expected, traveling almost twice as fast as the herd. If Stanton could hold out one more day, the old man and the boy would have him to where he could get help.

Hugo rode up fast and they dismounted to go over the ground in search of what they could read from it. But Tito Stanton had been before them. Hugo found the note wedged under a bark curl on the bole of a cottonwood tree.

"Weaker," it read. *"Couldn't get him out of the wagon. Amelio thinks fever worse, but no more fits.*

Midnight but a fair moon. Horses rested and holding up good. We're pushing on."

"Damn that old man!" Kinchloe growled. "He knows better if the kid don't. They hit a cutbank in the dark and that's all it'll take."

"I'd do the same," Hugo said. He paused a moment before adding, "So would you, I reckon."

Kinchloe was startled. The afterthought was the first concession of respect or confidence he had received from the black man. He nodded.

"I reckon," he agreed.

"We sure gave them the dirty end of the stick. Only his wife thinks any more of Spence Stanton than them two."

"Would you do it any different?"

"No, or I'd of done it," Hugo answered. "Let the good Lord help 'em for a few more hours. Me, I hope that Missouri nigger-hater catches up with us. I'd like to break his back with my hands for that lucky shot of his."

"Not me," Kinchloe said. "With these cattle on our hands I want no part of that son of a bitch!"

They remounted and rode back toward the herd. Raúl Archuleta was signaling them from far back on the drag. When they reached him, he had pulled up and was looking down their back trail. Kinchloe saw at once what troubled the *vaquero*. Almost full in the light path of the lowering sun and silhouetted against it was a knot of horsemen, following unhurriedly in their tracks.

Another knot of riders and then another appeared until fully thirty men were in view. Among their horses was a distinctively marked pinto which had been ridden from Pawnee Crossing and on the raid against the Dutchmen at Manykill.

"Well, it looks like you'll get your wish," Kinchloe said to Hugo. "Elijah Ames and his Missourians."

"Man, look at 'em," the black man said ruefully, shaking his head. "He's got a damn army. You sure called it right in sending the boss and the wagon on ahead. This may get a mite lively."

"And sudden," Kinchloe agreed. "Get into that draw up ahead. Ought to be a stream. Find us a loop in it big enough to hold the cattle if you can. Don't worry about wood. We won't be building any fires tonight."

Hugo wheeled and loped back up along the herd. The elder Archuleta resumed his place on the drag. Kinchloe remained motionless in his saddle, watching the party behind them. When a man understood this kind of business he could frequently predict the unknown intent of others by putting himself in their place.

Ames knew he had superiority in numbers. He also knew the Corona crew could sting. He had learned that at Manykill. He would exact his price for that. Retaliation was the nature of such men. But it was the cattle he was after. He would make sure he had them secure before turning full attention to wiping out any remaining witnesses.

That he would have to do if he was going to make his theft stick when he brought the cattle on to the river to sell.

There was some wry satisfaction in the knowledge that at least two and hopefully three from the Corona had already escaped him, so he would be undone there. But the important matter for the moment was what he would do here. He had made no attempt to conceal his approach and so surprise did not figure into his plan. Nor was he making any attempt to close with the herd and was instead holding his pace down to that of the cattle, so he had no intention to strike immediately.

It made for uncomfortable waiting, but afforded time for some counterplanning. Kinchloe was satisfied to accept that and wait the Missourian out. But one thing troubled him. Ames's recruit from Pawnee Crossing would have informed him of the size of the drover crew and the makeup of the drive. He would have already noted the absence of the chuck wagon and the fact the crew head count was three shy.

It was important to learn as soon as possible what he intended to do about that, if anything. Like Spencer Stanton himself had proved to be on occasion, Jack Kinchloe was impatient when others had the deck. Waiting was not his style when the choice of time and place was not his.

He rode back to the point of the herd, warning the *vaqueros* along the way to ignore the Missourians until they made some overt move. To all appearances, there was no alarm among the drovers, and they were accepting the party behind them as chance travelers overtaking them on the trail.

The cattle crested a low swell and slanted down into the draw beyond. A stream, a little smaller than Kinchloe would have liked for his purpose, meandered through a well-grassed meadow there. Hugo was riding along the stream bank in the largest and deepest loop in its course. Presently he signaled he was satisfied with the lie and Kinchloe turned the point toward him.

The herd followed the lead steer into the loop. The cattle spread out to water but none attempted to cross the stream and Kinchloe thought that it would hold them in spite of its small size. He put the cavvy of horses in behind the beef and detailed Benny and Ramón Archuleta as first-shift nighthawks to hold the open end of the loop closed. The rest of the hands he dismounted to rest themselves and their mounts.

The Missourians came over the crest of the swell and rode unhurriedly down to water about a mile upstream. Here they also dismounted and began collecting wood and setting up camp. Hugo and Raúl Archuleta came over to hunker down with Kinchloe. Both eyed their neighbors with little liking.

"They got to have figured by now that the chuck wagon and a couple-three of our boys have gone on ahead," Hugo said worriedly. "Seems like they'd ought to be doing something about that if they figure on keeping their noses clean at the river. Like sending some after it."

"Seems," Kinchloe agreed. "But maybe there's a better way to do it. Or no harder anyway."

"Like what?"

"They don't know why the wagon's gone on ahead. Probably think to start rounding up buyers or something. But they do know that there's only two or three men with it and one's Stanton. They're sure to have missed him by now. Likely the boy, too. Ames may figure to send a few into Leavenworth to take care of them after they've got the cattle. Makes sense. We're the hardest nut to crack."

"Could be," Hugo conceded uncertainly. "But damn 'em for making us sweat it out. And I ain't sure I like this pocket you got us in, crowded in tight against the creek."

"*Yo también,*" Raúl Archuleta agreed. "In the mountains we have much room, *señor*. Room to ride, to shoot, to herd the cattle. That we understand. But in such a little place like this, the water on three sides and the cattle behind us, I do not think we can make such a good fight maybe."

"We'll see," Kinchloe said. "Maybe you'll make a better fight than you expect — if they try what I think they might. Tell everybody to break out some grub and feed while there's still light."

The elder Archuleta moved reluctantly away, passing the word. Saddle rolls were broken open and men ate the rations parceled out by Amelio where they were. Just before dark six men rode downstream and passed the bedded herd about a quarter of a mile out onto the meadow. At that distance Ames was readily recognizable in the lead.

"Wants to make damn sure we know who we're up against, don't he?" Hugo growled. "Scouting us out, to boot."

"Going down below us to check out the wagon tracks, just to make sure it did light out for the river," Kinchloe said. "Tracks'll read out better'n a day old. That'll tell 'em all they want to know. They'll be back up directly."

Kinchloe's hunch proved correct. Ames and his men disappeared in lowering darkness back toward their camp. Presently three fires were kindled there. Kinchloe watched the flames for a few moments, then stood up, stretching the cramp from his legs.

"That does it," he said. "Pass the word, Hugo. Everybody make up their rolls again and saddle a fresh horse. Take the mounts back through the cattle to the creek and hold 'em there at ready. Tell Benny and Ramón to get the hell out of the open mouth of this loop at the sound of the first shot."

"What the devil you up to?" the black man demanded.

"Little surprise for our friends," Kinchloe answered. "Ames thinks he's got us trapped. He knows he's got us outnumbered in guns and so he has. But not in cattle. Get a move on. We ain't got all night!"

Hugo moved soundlessly away. Kinchloe found his saddle and retied his roll. Lugging his saddle by its D-ring he worked silently back through the bedded cattle to the creek at the deepest part of the loop and then returned for a fresh horse from the cavvy.

Others were doing the same with admirable silence. Kinchloe thought Hugo must have warned them convincingly. He led the horse back through the cattle to his saddle on the creek bank and swung the leather up. The steers were beginning to stir with the traffic through them. It was unavoidable not to spook them some and advantageous as well if it wasn't overdone. He could only hope the constant movement didn't make them too restless too soon.

He had another concern. The moon of which Tito and Amelio had taken advantage the night before had not yet risen, but he had himself been asleep when it rose the night before and he was not sure what time to expect it tonight. Light would spoil his plan.

Sounds of movement except among the cattle and the waiting horses presently ceased and he knew the Corona crew had their saddles up and were waiting about him. He mounted and heard others do likewise. One of them rode against his knee.

"Think they'll come tonight?" Hugo's voice asked softly.

"Any minute."

"What makes you so sure?"

"Those fires yonder. That's too much."

"Hell, man, it takes at least three fires for that many men to cook around them."

"Not their number; their size. They're too big. Only thing you could cook around them's your own damned hide. That's to make us think they're settled for the night so we'll settle too and they can ride right over us."

The black man grunted, almost inaudibly.

"You've rode a few miles, haven't you, mister?" he said.

"When I yell go, bloody your spurs, but don't overrun the cattle. Pass it along."

Hugo edged his horse away and spoke quietly to a nearby *vaquero*. Muted, the message moved on to others. More of the cattle were up now, moving restlessly. Kinchloe could hear the grunting complaint as still more heaved up. He tried to pierce the darkness toward the open end of the loop in the stream to see if he could locate Benny and Ramón Archuleta but he could not.

Time ticked by slowly. Kinchloe eased his rifle from its boot and made sure a cap was on the nipple. The long gun would be for his first shot. Thereafter it would be handgun work if his hunch was right.

Suddenly a shrill whistle sounded from where he had posted the Archuleta boys. It was almost immediately followed by the flash of a shot a little farther out onto the open meadow. There were shouts and a drum roll of hoofbeats as the Missourians abandoned their surreptitious approach and lashed up in a full charge.

"Let's go!" Kinchloe yelled. "Spook the hell out of those steers!"

He continued to yell unintelligibly and spurred into the first of the cattle. His horse was nearly jostled off its feet as one of the big Corona animals lurched up in front of it. Startled, heads up and snorting nervously, others were scrambling to their feet in sudden alarm.

All around him the Corona *vaqueros* were shouting and yipping, spooking the beasts up. A couple of guns banged again beyond the mouth of the loop in the stream but Kinchloe doubted they were yet close enough to have targets.

Under pressure from behind, the herd broke and began to run. The stream on either side held them in spite of its small size and they lumbered in a bawling, jostling mass toward the open end of the loop and the charging Missourians.

Kinchloe, who did not impress worth a damn in most things, was astonished at the speed of the stampeding animals, an irresistible river of horned flesh. He hoped the Archuleta boys had gotten clear, into the creek if necessary to keep out of the way.

The Missourians, now also hemmed in by the stream on either side as they entered the mouth of the loop, charged full into the onrushing cattle before they could realize what was happening in the darkness. The best drovers in the world could not turn so big and badly spooked a herd in so narrow a space.

It was pandemonium. Hoof rumble seemed to shake the ground. A horse screamed somewhere as it went down. Frightened men yelled hoarsely in alarm. Some shot senselessly into the thundering mass of cattle. Muzzle flame flared off to one side. Kinchloe thought it was one of the Archuletas and guessed the *vaquero* had found a close-quarter target as a raider fought free of the herd.

Then suddenly they were out through the mouth of the loop in the stream onto the meadow. Kinchloe spurred hard up from the rear alongside the stampeding herd, searching. Another man was close behind him. He thought it might be Hugo. He supposed others of Stanton's crew were also fanning up along both sides of the streaming river of steers, likewise searching for any of Elijah Ames's thoroughly broken up and scattered charge. The Corona *vaqueros* knew cattle. They understood this kind of work.

Shots were coming more often now as the disorganized Missourians began to regroup and recover from their shock and confusion. Two of them suddenly worked clear of the flank of the stampede, riding nearly into Kinchloe before they became aware of him.

Rifle level across his thighs, he shot the foremost through the body at almost point-blank range. The man went down and was lost in the night. Kinchloe jammed his rifle into its boot and jerked his belt gun, but the second man was past him before he could use it. He twisted in his saddle for a try anyway and saw whatever Corona hand was behind him knock the raider from his horse.

Kinchloe slowed and pulled up, realizing they risked overriding the scattered Missourians and missing them in the darkness. The man who had been behind him was Hugo. He pulled up alongside. They sat there tensely, listening to the stampede thunder past.

A faint glow was beginning to softly etch the line of the eastern horizon, throwing the tumbled, heaving heads and shoulders of the pounding steers into black silhouette. The moon was about to rise. Kinchloe's jaw hardened. Ames had cut timing that close. So had they. But it wasn't over yet. Not by a damn sight.

Two *vaqueros* came up warily, guns tensely at ready until they could identify Hugo and Kinchloe. The last of the stampeding cattle passed and strung on into the night across the meadows. More Corona hands materialized out of the dust. The Achuleta boys were doubled on one horse. Ramón had lost his and was smeared with the blood and dirt of a fall, but he still had his gun.

Pedro Lloras had a bullet burn across his cheek from the corner of his mouth to the lobe of his ear. The lower half of his face was a bloody mask. However, he was grinning as he held up two fingers to mark his count. He was ready for more.

Raúl Archuleta made a quick tally and reported two were missing. There was no time for further wait or search. As the sound of the herd faded Kinchloe could hear the hoofbeats of riders. They were bearing toward the false fires the Missourians had kindled on the creek. Kinchloe realized the Corona still held the advantage of surprise and he knew that it must be used while there was still opportunity.

"Vamos!" he yelled and set his horse at a flat run toward Ames's camp. The Corona hands streamed after him.

The fires in the Missourian camp had burned down considerably but their red glow was enough to throw fairly sharp silhouette. Kinchloe thought there were nearly a dozen men in the group they were pursuing, so several were as yet unaccounted for.

They rode hard, overtaking the Missourians as they approached their camp. With light to shoot against and blackness still behind them, Kinchloe pressed in close so as to be as certain of marks as possible. Every possible shot had to tally.

Suddenly, out into the meadow somewhere, Ames's voice roared out in stentorian bellow.

"You fools, stay away from that light! Over here, damn you. Over here!"

The men the Corona hands were pursuing

broke in belated realization and veered toward the sound of Ames's voice. Kinchloe swore and opened up. So did the *vaqueros* behind him. It was scattergunning at this distance and in this light, but three of the Missourians fell before darkness again swallowed them.

Chancing the risk for what it was worth, Kinchloe held to the fires. Vaulting down there he began pitching saddle rolls and whatever other gear he could quickly get his hands onto atop the flames. The Corona hands did likewise. In moments the camp was stripped.

Hitting saddle again, Kinchloe led the *vaqueros* back into the night, even as rifles opened up on them from the darkness of the meadows. They outrode this, driving after the slowing cattle, and he believed there was no pursuit.

The moon came. They rounded the head of the stampede and turned it in on itself so that the cattle milled and came to a frustrated and willing standstill. Leaving half the crew to hold the blown animals where they were, Kinchloe and Hugo took the rest and backtracked the stampede. There was no sign of those of Ames's party still up in saddle in the meadows. As daylight began to come on, it became apparent they had withdrawn somewhere over the swell of the prairie above the draw.

They found Ramón Archuleta's horse down with a broken leg and badly cut by the horns and hooves of the beef that had overrun it. They shot the injured animal and rescued Ramón's saddle and gear. It was trampled but yet serviceable.

Rafael Garcia was huddled behind a hummock near his fallen horse. He had a twisted ankle and a superficial wound in his thigh but was otherwise all right. Near him were the ragged remnants of two Missourians he had knocked from saddle. Their horses had apparently been carried away by the stampede. His saddle and gear were beyond salvage. A fellow *vaquero* took him up double and they went on.

The other missing Corona crewman lay with his feet in the stream almost at the mouth of the loop in the creek. He had been shot through the head from ear to ear. His horse also was missing.

The attack and stampede had also cost Spencer Stanton six prime steers probably dropped by the Missourians' initial fire, although it was difficult now to determine. All in all, Kinchloe thought they had not done badly by the *patrón* of the Corona. By the best count they could make, they had cost Elijah Ames eleven and possibly twelve men. Enough at least to bark the bastard's shins.

They returned in thin dawn light to the herd and found that the Archuletas and the rest, seeing them coming back without the pressure of pursuit, already had the cattle lined out in the beginning of the day's drive. Kinchloe was content to fall in behind the drag where he could keep watch to the rear. Hugo stayed with him.

"That's the way Spence woulda done it," the

black man said approvingly. "Make 'em drop their pants and kick 'em in the crotch."

"Maybe we went to the same school," Kinchloe suggested.

"You and Spencer Stanton?" Hugo laughed. "I doubt it like hell. Think them nigger killers'll track us for another whack?"

"If I was Ames I sure as hell wouldn't. I ain't that fond of lead in the belly and there's easier ways to steal a herd of beef than on the hoof."

The black man frowned without comprehension.

"Now I don't get that a-tall, mister."

"You will," Kinchloe said assuredly. "You will."

CHAPTER 11

Dr. Jed Magruder was not a sociable man on most occasions. He had enough reason for some dislike of his fellowman and his fellowman for him, as far as that went. But he had a taste for whiskey after supper to settle the day's dust and he did not like to drink alone. The taproom off the dining room below stairs was a congenial enough place and remained so until the small hours. But those occasions when he got drunk in public did his practice little good, which was scant enough under the best conditions.

For these reasons he tolerated Major Carew's haphazard visits. In fact he had perversely come to anticipate them and he grew impatient if the officer was overlong in coming down from the Army post a few miles upriver. The military medic was supercilious and condescending toward all things civilian and he was a staggering bore, but they did have the commonality of their profession. With sufficient effort a conversation could be contrived. It beat the hell out of sitting in solitary silence contemplating the four blank walls of his hotel room.

Tonight the major had furnished the bottle as he did on alternate visits. It was now empty and he never furnished two, claiming such generosity impossible on military pay. Dr. Magruder reluctantly went to the clothespress in the corner and brought out a reserve he had stashed among his shirts. Major Carew took it and poured himself half a tumbler. He sipped appreciatively and watched Dr. Magruder pour rather more into his own glass.

"Free advice," the major said. "You'll take on gout or a bilious liver or rot out your bladder if you keep on hitting it that hard. Professional warning, for what it's worth."

"Save it for your troopers," Dr. Magruder grunted. "May impress them. Sure as hell doesn't me."

The major shrugged.

"I'd hate to be a patient of yours along about now."

"Nonsense," Dr. Magruder said. "You got no faith in the Hippocratic oath. I'm at my best with a few fingers over half a bottle. Nerves of steel."

"Sure," the major agreed. He sipped again. "Shake anymore and you'll knock your front teeth out with that glass."

It was true. Dr. Magruder gripped the glass

with both hands and tried to suppress the tremor. He saw that Major Carew's well-manicured hand was as steady as a rock. He resented that. He wanted to say so. They were drinking his whiskey now. But before he could summon a satisfactorily caustic phrase, footfalls pounded in the hall outside the door, running its length from the head of the stairs.

They halted abruptly at the door and a fist pounded insistently upon it. Dr. Magruder irritably put his glass down. It had been months since anyone had aroused him at this hour. Medical emergencies in the taverns and streets of Leavenworth at night tended to be violent and more or less instantly fatal. The need most often was for an undertaker, not a doctor, drunk or sober.

"Who the hell is it?" he demanded.

"Dr. Magruder . . . Dr. Magruder!" a voice called urgently.

It was a young voice, that of a boy, taut and tremulous with stress. Dr. Magruder unsteadily scraped back his chair, crossed awkwardly to the door, recovered, and dragged it open.

The boy was a stranger, about fourteen. His clothing was rimed with the dust of far travel. So was his tense, white face. His eyes were wide with sleeplessness and fear. He was no different than any other frightened youngster in this hard and violent country except in one thing. He wore a belted gun any man along the river would be proud to possess. He wore it with ease and comfort, unconsciously making it a part of him.

Dr. Magruder recognized the deceptive ease even if he did not understand it. He had seen men who so wore their weapons. Dangerous men with cold eyes and friendless faces. More and more of them were crossing the river these days on private and nameless errands. Men for whom others stepped aside without bidding. But it was incongruous in one so young.

He saw also that the boy instantly recognized his own condition. Disappointment was in the eyes. The worry in them deepened. The pleading hope wavered visibly.

"It's my father," the boy said thinly. "His leg. Broke. Almost six days ago now. It's mighty bad and he's awful sick. They're bringing him in from the wagon downstairs."

"Who are you, son?" Dr. Magruder asked kindly in spite of himself.

"Robert Stanton."

"Well, Bobbie," Dr. Magruder said, "you just hang on a minute and we'll see what we can do about your daddy."

He picked up his bag from the foot of the bed. Major Carew faced him, seizing his arm.

"Good god, you can't treat an injured man in the shape you're in!"

"Wanna bet?" Dr. Magruder challenged, tugging his arm free.

"I forbid it," the major insisted. "That's an order."

"You, order me? Like hell."

137

"I'm coming with you then. I insist."

"Do that. See how a civilian works. May pick up a handy pointer or two. And bring that bottle. If the patient doesn't need it, I will."

Dr. Magruder dropped a hand to the waiting boy's shoulder and turned with him down the hall. Major Carew followed. With amusement Magruder saw that the Army man was obediently gripping the neck of the bottle from the table. The habit of command was not limited to the military alone.

There was a gaggle of the curious in the lobby at the foot of the stairs. They pushed through to the door of a ground-floor suite. Half a dozen men were clumsily easing a gaunt-faced, fever-shot man onto a bed in the inner room.

He was tall, well built in spite of the obvious wasting. His body was swathed in blankets and restrained with ropes. Against delirium, Magruder supposed. His hair was matted with sweat. A groan escaped him and Magruder realized he was conscious. A perfidious, ominous odor emanated from him. His color was ashen. He was a desperately stricken man.

Magruder shooed out the onlookers and voluntary stretcher bearers. One who persisted in remaining was an aged and crippled man of Spanish origin. The boy touched Magruder's arm.

"He is Amelio," he said. "He stays."

Magruder nodded assent. He caught sight of the night manager of the hotel in the outer room and called sharply.

138

"Get me a table in here. A stout one with a cover on it. All the extra lamps you can find. Some washbowls and all the hot water left in the kitchen. Get a move on, man!"

Major Carew had been bending over the man on the bed. He straightened, his nose wrinkling.

"Gaseous gangrene," he said without regard for the boy and the old man huddled together across the room. "Pulse racing and thready. God knows what fever. Too late, Magruder."

"We'll see. Give me that bottle."

The major obliged. Magruder took a long pull. The needings he had ordered were hustled in. The injured man was transferred to the table at a suitable height to be worked upon. More lamps were lighted and placed about wherever space for them to stand could be found. A steaming copper vat of water was lugged in. The night manager appeared with some towels and some white porcelain washstand bowls. Magruder pulled a sheath knife from someone's belt and started to slash the bindings restraining the injured man.

The cording was plaited rawhide and stubborn. Major Carew took the blade from him and made short work of the lashings. Together they peeled away the swathing blankets. The man's left leg was tightly bound below the knee and discolored above. The major cut away bandaging to reveal an ingenious wooden splint hand-carved to the contours of the leg. It was split apart longitudinally and came away in two halves.

Magruder examined this curiously and

dropped it into the vat of steaming water. Using scissors from Magruder's bag, the major expertly cut away inner bandaging to lay the injury bare. The break had been a nasty compound one and the resultant lacerations were putrescent. Despite the splint, attention given had been from amateur hands. The bone shaft seemed straight enough but Magruder could not tell if a satisfactory set had been made beneath the swollen, angry flesh. At this point it made little enough difference, he thought.

Major Carew peeled out of his jacket.

"Laudanum?" he asked.

"In the bag."

"Bone saw?"

The major rummaged and found the phial of laudanum. He handed it over.

"Maximum dosage," Carew said. "Even then we'll have to get a couple more in to help hold him. We'll take it off here, in good flesh above the swelling. It's the only chance and about as slim as they come at that."

His finger traced a dispassionate line across the injured leg about midway up the thigh. Magruder took another pull from the bottle.

"If we cleansed the wound carefully, cut out the proud flesh and repacked it well, maybe we could control the infection," he suggested.

"Hell, man, you know better than that," the major snapped, picking up the laudanum to measure out a dosage himself. "I've got no more stomach for it than you have. An amputation under these conditions. But he'll be dead by morning if we don't."

The man on the table opened his eyes. They were bright with fever but lucid. They jumped from Major Carew to Magruder.

"He right?" the injured man asked.

Magruder shrugged helplessly.

"Probably," he agreed. "They lose a lot of legs in the Army. He ought to know. It's just — well, hell, I just can't bring myself to take off a man's leg until I've tried everything else."

"Damn it, there isn't time," Major Carew insisted, "and we're wasting what little there may be."

The fevered eyes touched the bottle near Magruder and returned to him.

"How drunk are you?" the injured man asked.

"I've been drunker."

"Well, you save the rest of that bottle for me."

The eyes searched the room.

"Tito?"

The boy crossed quickly to the table, followed by the limping old man.

"Just you and Amelio?" the injured man asked.

"The rest are coming on with the cattle," the boy answered. "Here tomorrow, maybe. Or the next day sure."

"You'll have to do then. These doctors are going to have to give me a pretty hard time. Keep out of their way but watch them. If they change their minds or give up and start to take my leg off, shoot them. Shoot them both. Think you can do that?"

"Yes, sir," the boy answered with simple, sober assurance.

"So I figured, son," the man on the table said with a smile. "Don't worry. We'll make it. We always do on the Corona." He turned his head to Magruder and Major Carew. "All right, gentlemen, I'll take that laudanum now, with a whiskey chaser."

The next three hours were a sweating, stumbling nightmare for Dr. Magruder. The light was bad at best, the room increasingly and oppressively hot and stuffy from so many wicks alight. He was drunker and more unsteady than he dared to admit, even to himself. And the task before him was far more difficult than he hoped it would prove to be.

But his greatest problem was Major Carew. He badly needed expert help if not advice in the slow, meticulous work of separating tissue and searching out all flesh already dead or dying of infection. Nerves, vessels, ligaments, and muscle fiber had to be preserved to the greatest degree possible if the leg was ever to be usable again, even if he did by some miracle succeed in avoiding amputation.

To compound the difficulty further, the wound itself, although fairly extensive, was no larger than the splintered bone which had caused it in ramming to the surface. And he had to work around the bone itself without disturbing it in case a decent set had commenced.

However, Carew, who had been so ready to attack healthy bone and flesh farther up, would have no part of probing and excising in the festered flesh of the injury itself. He seemed as horrified by the operation as a student at his first dissection.

He seemed unable to anticipate Magruder's need for additional instruments or the necessity to cleanse those already in use frequently in a bowl of heated water. His face was pale in the lamplight and Magruder suspected him of an occasional wave of unprofessional nausea. In his state the Army man was worse than useless. Magruder thought he would have left without a by-your-leave except for a morbid fascination stronger than his aversion.

Carew's eyes flickered almost incessantly to the corner where the boy and the old Mexican man stood. They were tense and silent but kept back out of the way. Only when a fresh instrument was produced or there was a marked change in operational position did either shift. Even then it was only a readiness, not an overt move. But death was physically in the room. The boy had his orders. He would carry them out. If he was unable, the old man would attempt to do so for him. Magruder instinctively understood that. He thought that Carew, otherwise numbed by this experience, did so, too.

The most remarkable thing was the patient

himself. Magruder frequently winced at his own ineptness, knowing it cost the injured man needless additional and excruciating pain, particularly as time progressed and the opiate wore thin. But the phial had long since been emptied. Nevertheless there was no sound from the man on the table, even to a catch of breath.

There was no movement of nerve or muscle. Magruder had never encountered such a perfect discipline of body. After a while it came to him what the source of such strength of mind and body was. It was the measure of the affection this man had for the boy in the comer. He knew that what hurt him would hurt his son as much, and to save the boy suffering he would let no pain touch him.

Finally, probing deep beneath the bone with an instrument in each hand, Magruder suddenly felt a hard object. He turned his head over his shoulder to Carew.

"Forceps and a quarter-inch spatula," he said. "I've got something here, Major. For god's sake give me a hand."

Carew backed up, hands raised in protest.

"I told you I'm not getting into that mess. That much infection you could get septicemia from a hangnail. You're only stirring it up and driving it through his bloodstream."

"Damn it, I've only got so many hands," Magruder raged furiously.

Carew backed another step, shaking his head in stubborn refusal. Magruder carefully released the instruments in his hands, leaving them in place in the wound. He wheeled on the major then.

"You son of a bitch — and you called *me* drunk! Get hold of yourself. You're a doctor, aren't you?"

Swinging full-armed he slapped the Army man hard with open palms on one side of the face and then the other, rocking his head back and forth on his shoulders. The staccato sounds of the repeated blows came like pistol shots. Stinging color flooded Carew's checks and a little blood trickled from one nostril.

Astonishment swept the officer but his mood shattered and he made no protest. Magruder saw that the man on the table had opened his eyes.

"Somewhat of a heller, aren't you, Doc?" he asked wanly.

For the first time in their long, tense vigil the boy and the old Mexican in the corner looked at each other and smiled. Magruder angrily shook a balled fist under Carew's nose.

"Forceps and spatula," he repeated. "On the double. You showed me how steady your hands are. Now, goddamn it, prove it. I may have got at the root of the infection."

The major got the additional instruments from the bag. Magruder took them from him and indicated the instruments he had left in the wound.

"Hold them right as they are while I see if I can

145

slide in alongside and a little deeper."

Carew did as directed. Magruder saw with satisfaction that the major's hands were indeed rock-steady. He slipped the spatula and forceps into the wound, probing carefully. He felt the spatula strike the object he had felt before and lowered the forceps to it. They gripped. He gently eased the object from the tissue in which it was imbedded and withdrew it from the wound.

He placed it on the table cover before Major Carew. It was a splinter of bone the size of a small penknife blade. The honeycombed inner side where it had splintered away was badly discolored. In living tissue it was a foreign and poisoning substance. It had already begun to rot. The odor which came with it was proof of that.

"I'll be goddamned!" Major Carew said softly with the first touch of professional respect Magruder had ever encountered in him. "You're bushed. I'll take over for cleanup, Doctor."

Magruder nodded and stepped back. The major withdrew his instruments as well and began a careful swabbing out of the wound with a carbolic acid solution, working swiftly and efficiently. When the wound was clean Magruder approved and the major skillfully packed it. Shortly the curious but effective carved wooden splint was back in place, securely bound for support. Carew rinsed and dried his hands and offered one to Magruder.

"Congratulations, Doctor. That's the most

thorough and comprehensive excision I've ever witnessed, It was a privilege to be present."

Magruder took the hand.

"Thanks for the assistance," he said wryly.

"Shocking display of unprofessional behavior," Carew admitted. "Afraid we found out which one of us was drunk." He bent over the man on the table, whose eyes had reopened. "Mister, you're lucky the right man worked on you. That leg's going to give you some more hell yet, but it'll come along. I don't know how well, but you'll walk on it again."

At the door the major paused and looked back hopefully.

"Same time next week?" he asked Magruder.

"Same time," Magruder agreed. What the hell? He was company.

With the help of the boy and the old man Magruder moved the table and got the injured man down off of it onto the bed. They dragged the table and debris out into the lobby for the night manager to dispose of. Magruder spoke to the boy.

"You can believe the major, son. Your daddy'll be all right. You two can sleep in the outer room. Just leave the door open. If anything worries you, come running. Otherwise I'll see you in the morning. Good night, Bobbie."

"It isn't Bobbie," the boy said. "It's Tito. Good night, Doctor."

CHAPTER 12

Stanton's fever lowered progressively to normal. He slept prodigiously in great blanks of utter exhaustion between light meals Amelio brought from the hotel kitchen and Dr. Magruder's calls to change the dressing on his leg. He knew it had been a close thing. He knew it better than even either of the doctors had. But by returning appetite and the constant sleeping he knew he was beginning to mend.

Practicality forced him to devote his waking time to putting his mind to making the healing process as fast as possible. He refused to waste useless concern on the safety of his crew and the disposal of his cattle. In his present helplessness that was still for others to do in his place. So he ate and slept and waited with a patience that was hard come by.

Each time he opened his eyes Tito was sitting

on a bedside chair. A quick smile always greeted his awakening. Each warmed away a little more of the anxiety in the young face and eyes. That was a good sign, too. Tito also knew that death had passed close but the chill of that knowledge was fading as each passing hour made improvement obvious. Stanton was grateful for this. It was Tito who had suffered most.

Finally there came a time that Tito was not on the bedside chair when Stanton opened his eyes. He stood at the foot of the bed and Hugo was in his place. The black man's smile was as relieved as the boy's.

"Your pa sure whelped hisself one tough *hombre* when he had you, Spence," Hugo said. "You done the same with Tito. Kinch said him and Amelio'd get you here in time but the rest of us wasn't so damned sure."

"I wasn't taking any bets," Stanton admitted. "The boys?"

"Some wear and tear's about all."

"The cattle?"

"Penned against the river north of town. Kinch is seeing to 'em. That bastard sure don't squeak in a tight. He'll be along directly. You grab some more shut-eye till then. We can palaver later. Just wanted to say howdy for me and the boys."

Hugo got up from the chair. As he turned toward the door Stanton saw a raw fresh contusion on his cheek and a fleck of blood at the corner of his mouth that his swabbing hand had not quite brushed away.

"Hold on," Stanton said. "That's fresh blood. Trouble?"

"You could say," Hugo admitted with a wry grin. "On the way in. Damned hammer-headed horse run me into a tree limb when I wasn't looking. Had it coming, I guess. *Hasta la vista,* Spence."

The black man touseled Tito's hair in passing and went out. Tito smiled after him and returned to the chair. Stanton fixed a stern eye on his son.

"You got any notion why he'd want to lie to me?" he demanded.

Tito looked startled.

"Hugo lie — specially to you? He wouldn't. You know that, Pa."

"He wouldn't let the meanest bronc alive run him under a tree either," Stanton growled.

The cattle were strung out along the banks of the Missouri, loosely held by almost motionless *vaqueros.* The beeves seemed to understand the long trek was over. They were heads down, content to graze with a minimum of movement and drift. Kinchloe doubted cannon fire could stampede them now.

He sat with his back against the bole of a tree, watching the five well-dressed townsmen ride toward him. Like the cattle, Kinchloe was at ease, grateful that his task was nearly over. He had chosen his potential buyers well. A few discreet inquiries and the response had been eager. They had been riding from bunch to bunch among the animals for two hours. He thought a deal could be made without too much difficulty now that they had seen the merchandise. Tomorrow would wind it up.

Kinchloe did not rise as the five most important traders in Leavenworth rode up, forcing them to dismount and hunker down before him. He relished this as he did the power of a gun in his hand.

They appeared to have appointed a spokesman, the fat, florid senior partner of the firm of Oliver & Caldwell, reputedly the shrewdest businessman on the Missouri. The fat man was not comfortable on his hunkers and clumsily lowered his butt to the ground, finding himself no more comfortable in that position. He tried to make the best of it. Kinchloe relished that, too.

"I suppose your intent is to have the five of us bid competitively," Sam Oliver said. "Your principal's intent, rather."

"No," Kinchloe answered. "I told you Mr. Stanton's laid up and out of the dickering. It's up to me. All I want to do is sell his cattle for him at a fair price."

"Understand, Kinchloe, this is a new experience for us," the fat man said carefully. "Thirty-five head is a lot of beef. Here we got thirty-five hundred, give or take a few. No assurance we can move that many before they've ate the whole damned prairie down to the roots."

"Prime beef," Kinchloe said. "There's ways. You'll find 'em."

"Maybe so," Sam Oliver agreed. "But no assurance. So we've agreed to form a syndicate. Spread the risk among all of us. We'll be hard enough put to cover as it is. One bid, Kinchloe, take it or leave it. You see this Stanton understands that."

Kinchloe shook his head.

"You don't listen very good, mister," he said easily. "It's up to me. Just me."

"All right. Twenty-two dollars a head. As is and where is."

Kinchloe shook his head again.

"Afraid I didn't hear that. Try thirty."

"Preposterous, man!"

"They'll bring thirty-five in St. Louis."

"That's a long way, Kinchloe."

"So's New Mexico, but they made it here. They'll make it on down the river if they have to."

"Twenty-five. Not a cent more."

The other traders nodded corroboration. Kinchloe shrugged.

"You're forgetting something," he said. "There's plenty more out there where these came from. You won't get a chance to bid on the next Corona drive. It'll go to St. Louis in the first place. Spencer Stanton is like that. He's a big man in his part of the country. Bigger'n the lot of you. And tougher."

The men exchanged looks. Sam Oliver's

manner subtly altered.

"He can deliver thirty-five hundred head a year here?" he asked.

"For starters. Ten thousand later if your money's good enough."

"This Corona must be some ranch."

"It is."

Oliver looked at his companions again.

"Stanton'd give us an option on another thirty-five hundred head for next year?"

"At fifty cents a head. Thirty dollars and fifty cents and write your own terms."

Oliver heaved awkwardly to his feet. The others rose with him. They moved to the far side of their horses and conferred there. Kinchloe remained squatting on his heels, waiting undisturbed. Presently the group returned. Kinchloe knew he had won and came to his feet.

"Your last word, Kinchloe?" Sam Oliver asked.

"It is."

"You drive a hard bargain."

"A fair one, anyways. We tally at thirty-four hundred and fifty-six head. Make your own count if you're a mind. But put your own crew on 'em in the morning. I want to start Stanton's home. I'll be at the hotel with him."

"Take us till maybe noon tomorrow to raise the credit and figure out our shares. When we got that done I'll bring you a draft from the bank."

"Cash," Kinchloe said. "No banks in New Mexico."

"Good god, man, that's better than a hundred thousand dollars!"

"A hundred and five thousand four hundred and eight to be exact."

"Christ, there isn't that much gold in Leavenworth!"

"Gold?" Kinchloe asked mildly. "Near six hundred pounds of it? How you aim to carry it?"

"I hadn't thought of that," Sam Oliver admitted.

"I have," Kinchloe said. "Down to the last pound and ounce if you want. Paper money's what I want. Currency. Nice, crisp government notes. They travel easy and they got a long way to go."

"All right. By noon tomorrow."

"Good."

The traders returned to their horses and pulled themselves to saddle with the big-assed clumsiness of chair-sitting businessmen. They rode off down the river toward the smoke over Leavenworth. Half a mile down a rider passed them on the way up. Kinchloe saw it was Hugo and awaited his approach.

The black man had an ugly bruise on his cheek and his lip was swollen at one corner. Kinchloe frowned and eyed him narrowly.

"What the hell happened to you?"

"Our Missouri friends," Hugo said. "Few of 'em came out of a saloon with a head of steam up and caught me on the walk. Seems like they aimed to boot me off it."

"But they didn't, eh?"

"Not so's you could notice. But it wasn't for not tryin'."

"Ames with 'em?"

"Not then or I might have come off worse. But I seen him with some others later. He's sure here. Like you said. On the prod."

Kinchloe sucked in a sibilant breath of air.

"God damn it!" he breathed softly.

So it was not to be over yet, after all. He had been afraid of this but had hoped luck would outride it if he moved fast enough. Now there was one more task to perform for Spence Stanton and himself. Perhaps the most difficult. A man never knew, going in. Only coming out.

"See the boss?" he asked the black man. Hugo nodded. "How is he?"

"Worse than I'd like but better'n he's got a right, I suppose. He'll walk but not soon."

Kinchloe indicated the bruise on Hugo's cheek.

"Get that before or after?"

"Before."

"Tell him about it?"

"A little cock and bull. No use letting him and Tito sweat any more than they've already had to."

Kinchloe nodded.

"Best mind this ourselves. Up to going back to town?"

"With you?" Hugo rubbed the bruised cheek and smiled. "I think I'd like that just dandy."

"While I cinch up you ride over and tell Archuleta to hold the boys here till he hears from me. All of them. I don't want any drifting into town and getting all of our tails in a crack."

Hugo rode off through the cattle. Kinchloe crossed to his grazing horse. The saddle was up. He slipped in the bit, kicked a belch of air from the animal's belly and jerked the loosened cinch tight. Hugo returned as he swung up. Kinchloe saw that the black man had stopped by the duffel pile. A second pistol was thrust under his belt.

Neither made any comment and they rode knee to knee for town.

The streets of Leavenworth were deceptively quiet, the lull before the raucous pleasures of the night. The rays of the low-slanting sun were golden with motes of the day's dust in the motionless air. Very little traffic was out. Kinchloe held Hugo and himself precisely to the center of the street, riding at an unhurried walking trot.

These things had to be done exactly in a certain way in order to gain every advantage available. Small sights and sounds had their influence. Reflexes and instincts were stirred or allayed by small signals. Familiar patterns of movement and appearance could alarm or reassure according to tiny variations. All could work for a man or against him.

Two slatterns were airing themselves after the heat of the day on the steps of a cathouse. They eyed the two passing horsemen with practiced

156

glances. Without a word between them they rose, gathered their skirts, and went inside without the usual professional blandishments.

A group of four or five labor-soiled men were idling in the shade of an awning before a saloon. Their small talk broke off as Hugo and Kinchloe passed. However, they remained as they were and talk resumed in a moment. By this Kinchloe knew those he sought were not behind that pair of swinging doors.

They passed the hotel. Amelio was on the veranda. The old *vaquero's* eyes followed them but he gave no sign of recognition or awareness. Kinchloe thought Amelio knew and understood, so that would be all right. He was glad Tito Stanton was not with the old man.

A little farther on a man stepped briskly out of the dark maw of a livery stable as though on an errand. He stopped abruptly when he saw the two riders, turned on his heel, and ducked back within. Kinchloe glanced at Hugo. The black man nodded. A Missourian. You could smell the bastards.

Now as they rode, Hugo withdrew his left arm from its sleeve and rebuttoned his shirt over it with it against his belly as a man with a bad wing will do for want of a sling. Only now the black man's extra pistol was gripped in the hidden hand. It was not a thing Kinchloe had seen done before. Obviously Hugo had. A man learned strange lessons to survive.

At a corner was a large building with white-washed windows and batwing doors giving onto a walk and a long hitch rail along the side street front. Over a dozen saddled horses were racked there. Benches were occupied by another group of the usual saloon idlers. Two of these quickly stepped through the doors into the interior as Hugo and Kinchloe came around the corner. The rest moved away, hastily dispersing, as though their wives had called every last man home for supper at this instant.

Kinchloe knew then that this was where they were. Some of them anyway. Enough, he hoped. He reined to the rail and swung down. Hugo stepped down beside him, favoring his invisible arm and hand as though it pained him.

"Stay behind me," Kinchloe ordered. "No telling how this'll go. Wait it out. I'll use the whip. Just keep any off my back."

The black man nodded and they stepped across the walk to the doors.

CHAPTER 13

The saloon was deep but narrower than it had seemed it might be from the outside. The bar ran back the length of one wall. An irregular row of tables and a clutter of chairs were strung along the other. Barely more than a wide aisle from front doors to back lay between. Kinchloe was pleased with the restricted open area. It reduced the size of his target of attention.

Without a change in the brisk stride with which he had crossed the walk outside, Kinchloe went directly to the head of the bar. He bellied up to the short turn there at right angles to the long run down the room. In this position the bar itself shielded the lower portion of his body without impairing his full-figure view of those he faced. This, too, was part of the pattern, instinctive and automatic.

The gaunt, towering, white-bearded figure of

Elijah Ames was against the bar at a distance of five or six yards. His men were beyond him, behind him in effect, strung along toward the rear. There were eight of them, almost certainly none of them local townsmen.

Kinchloe saw that the door at the rear hung slightly ajar as though someone had recently made a hasty entry or exit by way of it. The men facing him were silent, all talk and movement suspended. They had been waiting for him and his companion. They had been warned of their approach. That also was as it should be and according to plan. To wait was to tense, and tenseness impaired both judgment and timing.

Kinchloe eyed the bartender briefly, deciding in that one glance that he was probably neutral and would remain so. However, as though to ensure this, he unhurriedly drew his right gun and openly placed it on the bar before him. The purpose was in fact different but that was the appearance.

The bartender reacted hastily. He backed from the bar itself against the back bar, nervously taking up a glass and a polishing cloth there. Kinchloe smiled, guessing the house man had been standing within reach of a scattergun under the bar. His guilty apprehension was self-evident. Kinchloe's eyes snapped back to the leader of the Missouri ruffians.

"We got to have a few words, Ames," he said quietly.

Piercing, wicked blue eyes peered out

unintimidated from under shaggy white brows.

"Verily, a prophet is not without honor save in his own country," the bearded man answered mockingly. "You have the advantage. You know my name but I don't know yours."

"You know the name. Everyone does. Jack Kinchloe. We've met before. Twice. This'll be the last time."

The icy eyes narrowed slightly. There was no other reaction.

"What's your business with me, a simple servant of the Lord?"

Without shifting his glance, Kinchloe's head tilted toward Hugo, whose breath he could feel close behind him.

"Some of your tarheeled disciples roughed up this rider of mine an hour or two ago. Up the street. We'll have satisfaction for that."

"Will you, now?" the Missouri Prophet sneered. "You lie before God, sinner. We're peaceful men, abiding our own business. Every soul on the river knows no man who rides with 'Lige Ames would get within spittin' distance of a stinkin' runaway nigger, let alone lay hand to him except for the law of the land and a white man's Christian rights."

"Rights, yes. I suppose that even jackleg bastards like you and yours are entitled to some. So I'll give every man in this room his chance."

Kinchloe slowly thrust the gun on the bar before him out a little farther. He saw that Ames pretended to ignore the weapon but his eyes were warily riveted upon it, waiting for the first signal of a stabbing reach. So were those of the others. It was curious how effectively so simple a device worked. Kinchloe had never known it to fail.

"I know what you're here for," he continued softly. "I aim to prevent it. Every man of you is free to go. Out to your horses and out of town. Send word to any others scattered around. Get and stay gone. Do that and we got no quarrel."

"A man of God has no quarrels except those thrust upon him," the bearded man answered defiantly.

With his eyes fastened on the gun on the bar top and the hand expected to streak for it, Ames smoothly and confidently lifted his own ponderous piece from its holster. He was faster than Kinchloe would have supposed. Nevertheless it was preposterously easy to leave his right hand momentarily motionless beside the bar-top gun, where all eyes were upon it, and to snap his left up from below line of vision to counter level.

He shot the Missouri Prophet squarely between the eyes. The great, gaunt man fell outward as a tree cut to heartwood and crashed heavily to the floor. Afterward it was not so easy. Ames's men, as preagreed among them, opened up at that first shot. Splinters flew from the bar top, stinging like bird shot as they struck.

The smoke of black powder at close range roiled up in a confusing screen. Kinchloe had the gun before him also up now, using it alternately

162

with that in his left hand for but one purpose —
to destroy as much flesh as possible in the brief
fragment of time allotted him.

He felt himself hit and then hit again. He
leaned against the bar and retained his feet. His
feeling of coordination and target, those finely
honed instincts that alone lay between him and
ignominious death remained intact. Gunfire
suddenly jolted behind him. He wheeled around,
backing against the wall where the angle of the
bar joined it.

His shirt afire from the muzzle flame of the
hidden gun firing from within it and his other
gun in his exposed hand, Hugo was swiftly emptying both at three men who had burst in
through the batwings from the street. With the
clear perception a man sometimes has in a shattered instant of time, Kinchloe recognized the
Missourians' strategy and the significance of the
gaping back door.

Ames had sent these three out that way to
circle to the street and come in behind the black
man and himself when it was known they were
approaching. Kinchloe was angry. He should
have anticipated that.

He swung his guns toward them but it was un-
necessary. They were already dead on their feet.
Hugo stepped back as they crumpled and fell.
Slapping at the fire in his shirt and snuffing it,
the black man came to Kinchloe. He burst his
pinioned arm free and thrust it back through the
ruin of its sleeve. Blood was on his torso.

"Whooee!" he breathed. "Pretty damned good hoedown while she lasted."

He indicated the room. Only the bartender remained on his feet. The back door now gaped wide. Kinchloe didn't know how many had escaped through it and he had no desire to make a count. Every man had a superstition about some things. What had to be done had been done. Best to let it go at that.

"I need a drink," he told the bartender.

"Me, too," Hugo agreed. "I'll pour my own."

"I'll serve," the houseman said in a scratchy, unsteady voice. "Proud to."

"Six men in less than as many seconds, the way Willie's telling it at the Redeye," Dr. Magruder said as he worked, "Including woolly old 'Lige Ames and some of the worst that run with him. Only a couple bullet burns and a little old pinky hole in the side meat between the two of you to show for it."

The doctor turned to Stanton.

"If the rest of your outfit's as cobby as you and this pair, I hope the lot of you stick around Leavenworth a spell. Good for my business. I can use it."

Stanton looked at Hugo and Jack Kinchloe. Their superficial wounds were now bandaged. Tito and Amelio were looking at them, too. Tito's admiration was obvious. Stanton thought that even Amelio's stubborn, long-standing mistrust of Kinchloe had evaporated.

"If you're finished, Doc —" he said.

"Don't rush me," Magruder protested. "I know I'm not going to be able to keep you down on your back like this as long as you ought. I want to take some measurements off that Dutch splint. A notion I've got."

Magruder flung back the quilting and put a pocket rule to the lower part of the halved splint, jotting down notes.

"A Goddamned carpenter," he complained. "Hell of a way to practice medicine."

Presently he replaced the quilting.

"All right?" Stanton asked.

"Christ, how do I know? It's *your* leg. All right? Godalmighty, no! But maybe it'll make do. We'll see. We'll see."

"Clear out, all of you," Stanton said irritably. "I want to talk to Kinch. Alone."

Magruder picked up his bag and left. The others followed him. Tito, the last, closed the door behind them. Stanton carefully shifted his splinted leg to a more comfortable position, grunting testily at his own awkwardness. Kinchloe sprawled back in his chair.

"Look, Stanton, before you open your yap, don't start woodshedding me," he warned. "It ain't your right under our agreement and I'm still a mite on the prod."

"I don't doubt it," Stanton growled. "Damned foolishness. You and Hugo both."

"They had it coming. It had to be done."

"Bullshit!" Stanton said. "Sure, they jumped

you and the herd out this side of Manykill. But you cost them enough out there to make them back off and leave you be the rest of the way in."

"You complaining?"

"Not about that. Good work, Kinchloe. What galls me is why open it up again here after the herd's delivered — sold, if your deal sticks together — and we've already taken our lumps?"

"One damned good reason. My job wasn't done. Thing like that's important to me if to nobody else."

"Soul of honor."

"Hell, no. Plain practicality. Ames has had everything going pretty much his way in this part of the country. He found out it'd cost him dear to hustle your cattle on the hoof. But come tomorrow or the next day at the latest you're going to have better'n a hundred thousand dollars delivered to you right in this room. That's something else. One man could walk away with that in a little old satchel."

"If he could get his hands on it."

"Easier'n you think. There's a lot in this town don't cotton to color. Any color different than their own. They don't give a damn what happens when they're not looking. Any kind of a damn at all. Niggers or greasers — or New Mexican ranchers — who gives a hoot in hell? No skin off their noses."

"So?"

"So you're flat on your back and they could

bushwhack me. In a couple days Ames and his bunch could clean you out of hands to the last man and not a finger raised. No trick to grabbing that satchel then. That's why they started with Hugo this afternoon, first chance they got. They had to be stopped before they had another. Better to risk two men at once than the whole outfit, one at a time."

"Not in my book," Stanton said doggedly.

"Oh, goddamn it, Stanton!" Kinchloe exploded. "Just how many men are you willing to trade for the take from those cattle?"

"That's just it, Kinch. I lost one man when Ames hit you out there on the grass. A couple more got bent up. That's enough. More's not worth it. They call me *patrón* out there. Sooner or later I got to face their families."

"Then get them to hell out of here before something else happens. This ain't their country and nobody's going to let 'em forget it. You're going to be here for weeks — two–three months or more, maybe. They'll be prodded and pushed till something gives. Keep your boy and the old man to look after you if you want. But send the rest back where they belong. Hugo and Raúl will see they make it without barking any more hide."

Stanton studied Kinchloe. There was no mistaking his urgent earnestness. By any standard by which a man could be measured he had proved himself. And he was right. The responsibility was there. It had to be faced, however much Spencer Stanton wanted to return in triumph from this drive, boss and crew intact.

"I'll do better than that, Kinch," he said slowly. "Tomorrow too late?"

"None too soon," Kinchloe said. "If they was my men. Sam Oliver's outfit's taking over the herd in the morning. It's his headache from there on."

"Fetch Hugo and Amelio and Tito back in."

Kinchloe went to the door and called. The three came in from the outer room, eyeing Stanton in curious uncertainty.

"Bring me my wallet," Stanton told Tito.

Tito handed it to him. Stanton undid the ties of the worn buckskin envelope. Its pockets were still heavy with minted gold. He divided their contents into three portions, giving one to each.

"You're starting home tomorrow," he said. "All of you. Between Doc Magruder and the hotel I can get all the help I need. Soon as I can travel I'll take the stage. I won't be too far behind you."

He held up his hand as all three started to protest.

"Amelio, grub up the wagon while there's still light and take it out to camp tonight so you can make an early start without anybody in town the wiser. These are orders, understand?"

The old man nodded and pocketed his portion of the gold without comment, but strong disapproval smoldered in his eyes.

"Hugo, guns, powder, caps; whatever else you think is necessary. And presents from me for

'Mana and Quelí and the baby. Pretty woman things to tide them over till I get home. You'll know what's best. You and Raúl will ride boss."

"You'll need one of us, Spence, till you're on your feet," the black man protested.

"The *vaqueros* will need you more. See they all make it. In health. That's an order, too."

Hugo accepted his share of the gold. Stanton turned to his son. It was a difficult thing to do.

"Tito, pass out as many double eagles as will go around to every man. Let them choose how much they want to spend and what they want to take home. They can give Amelio the money and he can make their purchases while he's buying for the chuck wagon."

"Yes, sir," the boy said. "But I'm not leaving, Pa. I'm staying with you. You promised we'd come back to the Corona together, the way we started out."

"Some promises we can't keep, however honest the intent," Stanton said. "You *are* going, just like the rest, because I'm ordering you to. Not because I don't need you here and want you. I do. You're going because you have the hardest job to do and you're the only one who can do it."

"No, Pa," Tito said with a strangely sounding echo of the inflexibility in Stanton's own voice when he was determined.

"Son, no man on the Corona in your lifetime has ever said no twice to a direct order from me. We'll not let it start now. You hear?"

Stiffly, silently, Tito nodded.

"You'll have to make your mother and sister understand that I'm all right, that there's nothing for them to worry about, that I'll be home soon, as fine as ever. You're the only one they'll really believe. That you'll have to do for me because this time I can't be there to do it for myself."

Tito looked at him for a long and difficult moment, then picked up the money before him on the quilting, pocketed it, and left without a farewell or even a backward glance. Hugo and Amelio exchanged troubled glances and shifted awkwardly, ill at ease.

"We better get a move on, too, Spence," Hugo said. "Plenty to do afore sunrise. Take care of yourself and don't worry about us or the family. We'll see to 'em and be waiting for you at the grant."

"I'm counting on that, Hugo. Good luck to you all."

"*Sí, para tu también, Patrón,*" Amelio returned. "*Buena suerte y bien salud.*"

"*Como siempre,* old friend."

The two *vaqueros* filed out after Tito, hurrying to overtake him. Kinchloe was sprawled again in his chair. He shoved his hat back and thrust his hands deep into his pockets.

"You are somewhat of a son of a bitch, Stanton," he said. "I suppose you know that."

"What brought on that sterling comment on my character?"

"I never had a kid. That I knowed of anyways.

Nor wanted one, for that matter. But I've come to set quite a store by that young one of yours. I hated to see you gravel him that way."

"I'd mind my manners, Kinchloe. An order's an order."

"Oh, Christ, don't feed me that! He's your son, damn it, not some ten-dollar hired hand."

"No difference, if he's been told to do something."

"Can't you see he practically worships you? Here you've had him about to pop his buttons ever since I joined up with you by treating him like a man and expecting everybody else to do the same. Now you got to break his heart by shoving him back into short pants and bundling him off back home without even a sugar tit to suck."

Stanton was uncomfortable and irritated. Kinchloe was prodding at a tender area.

"God damn it, if you're getting at something, get at it!" he demanded.

"You could have kept him with you. You know how much it meant to him. Should mean as much to you."

"I'm taking it that you mean well, Kinch," Stanton said with an effort to be reasonable, "so I'll tell you something. Something by your own admission you've never had a chance to find out for yourself."

"If it's about the boy, I wish to hell you would."

"If a *patrón* has a responsibility toward his *vaqueros* what kind of a responsibility does a father have toward his own flesh and blood? You're the bastard who talked up the dangers and mood of this town.

"A son of a bitch, you called me. Wouldn't I be a real one to send a crew of grown men home to keep them out of trouble and keep a fourteen-year-old boy here when I'm flat on my back and he'd be on his own for weeks or months, just because it would please me to have him with me?"

Kinchloe pulled his hands from his pockets and leaned forward with his forearms across his knees.

"Well, now, Spence, you got me there," he said. "Just never thought of it that way. Reckon you ain't quite the hardhead I figured and I apologize. Like I said, I never had a kid of my own and I was just trying to stick up for the boy. Think I'll go buy me a drink."

"Do that. Have one for me, too. Then get on out to the camp and see they get started as soon as Sam Oliver's crew shows up to take over in the morning.

"And another thing you haven't looked to. Have them cut enough of the best horses out of the cavvy so each man'll have a spare. They won't be working cattle and any more'd slow them down. See if you can sell the rest to Oliver or somebody. Let me know soon's they're on their way."

Kinchloe came to his feet.

"Yes, sir," he said meekly in a fair imitation of

Tito's tone. "Orders is orders. See you sometime in the morning."

Kinchloe left. Stanton reached under the bed for the bottle of whiskey Amelio kept there for him. He drank deeply and eased heavily back onto his pillows. His leg hurt and he wanted to sleep.

CHAPTER 14

The chambermaid brought Stanton's breakfast. It did not seem as good as when Tito or Amelio supervised its preparation. A reflection of his own mood he supposed. At any rate he was hungry and ate ravenously.

Dr. Magruder came in a little later. As was frequently the case at this hour he was a little hung over. He filched Stanton's whiskey from beneath the bed and rinsed the hair of the dog that bit him from his mouth and throat.

The medication seemed to improve his spirits. He began to hum unmusically to himself as he attended to Stanton's leg. It was an irritating habit in which he frequently indulged. Stanton thought it doubly so this morning but held his peace with grumpy effort.

Magruder spent more time than usual with examining and redressing the injury. He took more measurements with his pocket rule from the cast before rebinding it and helped himself to another drink.

"The major was down from the fort again last night," he confided. "Unexpected, the bastard. But he fetched the whiskey, so naturally I had to be hospitable. Wasn't easy, even then. Had a hell of a time keeping him from coming down and awakening you after midnight to see how you're coming along. Civilian's word isn't worth a damn with the Army. Bullheaded. No wonder the Indians whip their ass off whenever they get a halfway fair chance."

"Professional jealousy," Stanton said sourly.

"I'm entitled," Magruder boasted placidly. "Sheer genius. Infection's gone. We've got as fair a set as anybody could hope for under the circumstances. Bone's knitting. Wound's healing from the bone out, the way it should. Really damned little muscle damage, considering. We'll have you on your feet a sight sooner than I'd have thought possible."

"How soon?"

"Crutches in a month, maybe. A cane in two more. If I can keep you from doing some damned fool thing like lighting out for home before you're ready."

"You're going to have to do better than that, Doc," Stanton growled. "There's a pistol in yonder drawer. One of these mornings I'm going to get out of this blasted bed and put it to your head. Pretty damned soon now."

Magruder looked at him owlishly as he closed up his bag.

"Know what?" he asked thoughtfully. "I'll go to hell if I don't think you would."

"Don't stall around till you find out."

Magruder laughed. He picked up the whiskey bottle, again without invitation, and took a pull from it.

"No need to change the dressing twice a day now," he said. "Save wear and tear on your disposition and mine. I'll see you tomorrow morning sometime. And you stay put or I may use that pistol myself."

Magruder let himself out. Time passed slowly and Stanton's impatience and dissatisfaction rose. He tried moving the leg experimentally. Pain dissuaded him in a few minutes. He looked at the whiskey left in the bottle and decided against it, steeling himself to the task of waiting.

It was nearly noon when Kinch arrived. He carried a small bundle. Stanton glowered at him.

"Where the hell you been?" he demanded.

"Errands here and there," Kinchloe answered. "This is a pretty big deal for Leavenworth that we got going. Sam Oliver and his partners is having trouble getting their paper work done."

"I thought the deal was set."

"It is. I thought there might be some problems the way they dragged their feet while I was dickering with 'em, but not now. Once they got their crew on the herd this morning and knew what they had, they started arguing among themselves

176

how big a share each of 'em was going to take. They're down to the Redeye thrashin' it out now. I'd say it'd take 'em three–four more quarts to come to what you might call an amicable agreement. Sometime late this afternoon, I reckon."

"The hell with bastards that can't make up their minds," Stanton said testily. "The crew get off like I ordered?"

"What do you think, with Spencer Stanton giving the orders? Stores all stowed. Two horses to a man. Oliver's outfit'll take the rest. They took out about an hour after daylight, heading due west. They're traveling light enough to travel fast. What — ten or twelve days home, maybe? Time I got done with Oliver and his outfit and headed in here they was already out of sight over the skyline."

"No sign of trouble from what's left of 'Lige Ames's Missourians?"

"No. And no sign of them. Scattered. Back into their prairiedog holes. They got the word, all right. Like I figured they would if they got bit hard enough. But Sam Oliver and his partners had to do a little sweet-talking to keep my butt off a hot rock over that. And Hugo's. Even some talk about holding you responsible there for a bit.

"Seems they can't keep a marshal here long enough to do much good, but they got some kind of a town council or something. Safety in numbers, I reckon. A few didn't like seeing the undertaker get overworked that way. Eased off when Oliver convinced 'em Hugo was already gone and I'd be on my way as soon as the deal for the cattle's wound up."

Stanton nodded grudging satisfaction. As Kinchloe had earlier said, when the stakes were high, what had to be done had to be done. That was the law in the high country as it was here. He had no qualms over it in the face of necessity. And he had supposed Kinchloe would be able to suppress any outrage over the sudden deaths which had swept the Redeye Saloon. The man knew his trade.

That was not what troubled him. He did not want to beg for it. It was too close to him. Still he had to know.

"Any message for me from out there at the camp this morning, Kinch?" he asked.

Kinchloe looked puzzled, as though he did not quite understand. Stanton swallowed his pride.

"Tito, I mean. Did he send me any word?"

"Well, yes, I guess he did. Not word, exactly. He sent you this."

Kinchloe unwrapped the bundle he carried. It contained Tito's Mexican belt and holstered gun. Even the cap box, shot pouch, and powder canister were attached. The sum total of his father's gift.

"He said that since you didn't need him he didn't need this and wasn't entitled to it. Something like that. Wasn't easy said. He walked right away."

"That's all?"

"That's all. He got on his horse and never looked back."

Stanton nodded heavily.

"Put it in the drawer yonder with mine. Stop by the kitchen on your way out and have them send in my dinner. Be sure you're back with Oliver and his partners before supper tonight. I want to get this over."

Kinchloe reappeared with Sam Oliver at dusk. Kinch was in a spanking new outfit. It was suiting and of a different cut than he usually wore. Fancy, from wide-brimmed white planter's hat to gleaming patent boots. He had been to a barber for a trim and shave and a bath. Only the belted guns beneath the side-vented skirt of his coat remained the same. Stanton saw he carried a wrapped package which could only contain a pair of bottles of whiskey. He was curious but said nothing.

Oliver gripped a small carpetbag with a stout leather handle and heavy brass fittings. It was well laden. Kinchloe introduced the trader to Stanton. The hand that gripped his was eager and deferential.

"My partners have authorized me to conclude our transaction, Mr. Stanton," Oliver explained. "In view of your recent unfortunate injury, we thought too many visitors might tire you unnecessarily."

"Very considerate."

"They asked me to convey how honored we all

feel to be recipients of your ranch's first business on the river. A very important occasion, sir. The first Western beef. We hope it will become an annual trade with increasing mutual profit for us all."

"No reason it can't be. The Corona will have the cattle. I can guarantee you that."

"So Kinchloe assured us," Oliver said. "You will forgive the delay this afternoon, I hope. Some details to work out. And so large a sum in currency was difficult to raise on short notice."

"Hardly necessary," Stanton said. "Your bank's draft woud have been sufficient."

"Not for me, Spence," Kinchloe cut in. "The only time I trust a bank's when I've got a gun shoved through the wicket. I'm leaving tonight and I want my cut in spending money. That's why I specified cash. Till mine's been counted out, anyway. All right?"

Stanton shrugged. "No difference. It's all money. You're handling the deal."

"Good," said Oliver, obviously relieved. He unlocked the carpetbag and opened it, revealing the thick, banded sheaves of government notes crammed within. "The entire sum is here, including payment for the surplus horses we agreed to take this morning. You or Kinchloe will wish to count it for verification, of course."

"Why? You took our tally and didn't count the cattle. You're honorable men. So are we."

"Very gracious, Mr. Stanton. A handsome gesture. It would take considerable time, I fear."

180

Sam Oliver produced a paper from his pocket. "Thanks to you, I believe all that remains is your signature on this receipt acknowledging that the money has been delivered into your possession."

Stanton shifted over nearer his bedstand and signed the document. Oliver folded it, returned it to his pocket, and put the key to the carpetbag on the stand.

"A pleasure to meet you, sir," he said, rising. "May your recovery be speedy. My associates and I will call on you as it progresses. Meanwhile, if we can be of any service to you during your enforced stay in Leavenworth, you have but to let us know. A good evening to you both."

At the door Oliver paused.

"That's a very substantial sum of money, Mr. Stanton. Leavenworth, as you have discovered, is not yet as civilized as we might wish. Without your drovers you are severely handicapped by your injury. More so when Kinchloe leaves.

"Adolph Kemmerer, our largest banker, lives here in the hotel. The next floor, front. I took the liberty of asking him to stand by this evening in case you might wish to place the remainder in his safe after you've made your settlement with Kinchloe. He will be glad to oblige."

"Thank you," Stanton said. "Very thoughtful. Good night."

Oliver nodded and went out. Kinchloe looked after him speculatively.

"Funny thing, Spence," he said. "Ever notice there's two sides to every bastard you meet, no matter who he is? Take that one. Butter wouldn't melt in his mouth tonight, now he's got his deal and likes it. But yesterday, when we was dickering, he just about as sweet as a rattler with his buttons busted off."

"Some'll fool you," Stanton agreed.

Kinchloe sauntered over to the open carpetbag which Oliver had placed on the commode. He lifted out a sheaf of notes, tossed it in his hand, then dropped it back.

"One head in twenty," he said. "Five percent of the whole take. Damned good deal I made with you, even if I do say so. Fifty-five hundred dollars, give or take a few."

"Seemed fair then. Still does."

"Know something, Spence? I been around. Had my good luck and bad. High on the hog or down on the hocks. But I never had that much money at one time in my life before."

Stanton was belatedly beginning to realize that it was all over. The long haul was done. He had accomplished what he had set out to do. Not in the way he intended, but he had accomplished it. He owed this man much.

"You've earned it, Kinch. And a bonus. A thousand to boot."

"That wasn't the agreement."

"Is now."

Kinchloe shook his head wryly.

"You are something, mister," he said. Stanton recognized the genuine admiration in his voice. "Maybe that's what it takes to be a *patrón*."

"Put it this way," Stanton answered. "I couldn't figure you out for a long time. Just couldn't be sure. Maybe until tonight, even. It's my way of saying I'm sorry about that." He indicated the open carpetbag. "Go ahead, man. Count it out. Waiting's hard. I know."

Kinchloe closed the satchel, carefully snapping the lock shut.

"Not when you know it's there," he said. "A celebration first."

He unwrapped the whiskey he had brought and set it out, finding two tumblers on a shelf of the commode. He poured each half full and handed one to Stanton.

"I been planning this," he continued. "I told the cook to send a special supper in. Just the two of us. I'd intended Tito and Amelio, too, if you hadn't shipped 'em off with the rest." He raised his glass. "To the end of the drive."

Stanton's feeling of accomplishment and relief and gratitude was rising. He smiled.

"I'll drink to that."

They drank. Kinchloe replenished the tumblers.

"Look, now, damn it, when you get home you make it right with that young 'un of yours, Spence," he said earnestly.

"I will," Stanton promised, more fervently than he intended.

"Good. Him and me really hit it off. You don't take it unkindly that I showed him somewhat about that gun of his?"

"No. He needs to learn, out where we come from. You're a good teacher."

"Likely none better," Kinchloe agreed without vanity. "He'll be the same one day. Damned if I don't miss him already."

Kinchloe frowned thoughtfully.

"I expected Doc Magruder."

"Not till morning. He thinks once a day's enough now."

"A good sign, I reckon."

"It had damned well better be."

There was a rap at the door. The hotel cook herself rolled in a portable supper table and snugged it up against the side of Stanton's bed. It bore a cloth cover and candles and a pink-rare roast of venison with a golden pastry pudding rising from the pan juices. Even an incongruous magnum of champagne. Kinchloe hitched his chair up to the other side of the table and pushed this last to Stanton.

"You do the honors, Spence. Only time I ever tried I blowed the damn stuff all over the room and wound up with nothing but an empty bottle and a lovely little lady madder'n a wet hen and soaked to the skin. It didn't hardly pay."

Stanton chuckled. He loosened the wire binder, cut the wax seal with it, and coaxed the cork gently with his thumbs. It freed with a satisfactory explosion and hit the ceiling but there was no spill from the neck of the smoking bottle. He poured into table stemware. Kinchloe raised his glass in another toast.

"To the Corona."

The wine was good. Better than Stanton remembered. It was pleasing to savor the once familiar taste again. The supper was also excellent. They ate slowly, relishing it, and talked little. Finally Stanton leaned back against his pillows, sated, a euphoric feeling of well-being permeating him. A flunky came and trundled away the table. Kinchloe produced cigars.

Stanton was half through his, enjoying the sensuous flavor of a fine Virginia wrapper before he began to realize his feeling of peace and contentment was more malignant than a mere sense of well-being. Not only was his injured leg immobilized without the usual nagging awareness of mild pain and discomfort but he was losing tactile sensation and control in his other members. His speech was thickening and he had great difficulty holding in focus the form and color of objects across the room. Kinchloe's face and figure wavered before him.

Stanton tried to sit back up accusingly but he could not.

"You son of a bitch," he said, enunciating carefully, "you aimed to do this from the beginning!"

"More or less," Kinchloe admitted easily. "Too good a chance to pass up."

He leaned forward, took the key to the carpetbag from the bedstand, and dropped it into his pocket. Stanton tried to intercept the move but Kinchloe easily evaded his slow, groping reach.

185

"You fired that shot into our camp the night you rode in."

"To convince you that you needed me," Kinchloe agreed. "Man like you takes a little persuading."

"The McAuslands — the three men you shot down on the street at Pawnee Crossing — they weren't after the herd."

"Just to turn you back, like they said. But you needed more convincing."

" 'Lige Ames and his Missourians in the saloon yesterday," Stanton continued, fumbling infuriatingly fuzzy thought into thick-tongued words. "They weren't rousting my *vaqueros.*"

"There you're wrong, Spence," Kinchloe corrected imperturbably. "Wrong as hell. They sure as the devil intended to. For the same reason I wanted your outfit started home. To get them to hell out of the way."

Kinchloe came to his feet. Stanton hazily saw that he had the handle of the carpetbag in his hand.

"Ames wanted what's in this satchel as badly as I do. It was him or me."

"You murdering, thieving bastard!"

"Come on, Spence, don't take it so hard. Nothing personal. You're a big man. You got your ranch to go back to. Family, hands, house. Cattle breeding you money all over the damned Territory. It's once in a lifetime for me. Be a fool not to take it. Whatever else I may be, I'm no fool."

"No man, either," Stanton accused. "You'd

186

have let Tito and Amelio stay. Figured on them for this celebration, even."

"Why not? Told you I got a feeling for your boy. It's true. Didn't want to see him hurt like he was. What the hell could a crippled old man and a boy do, once they'd sat table with us? Nothing. Like you."

Stanton grimly realized he was fighting a losing battle against the waves of numbness overtaking him.

"Something in the drinks — the food —" he mumbled.

"Drops Willie specializes in down at the Redeye. If they're still hanging on, Doc Magruder can give you something for them when he comes by in the morning. By then I'll be rich and long gone."

Kinchloe came close to the bed, bending over a little as though anxious his words be heard and fully understood. Stanton made a violent effort to seize him, to get his hands upon him, but the struggle was within his dulled mind only. His body refused to obey the command. He swore savagely but his lips did not move and there was no sound. No longer could he see.

"I mean you no harm," Kinchloe's voice said. "Believe that, Spence. We could have been friends. Great friends maybe. If you hadn't sold so damned many cattle. If you weren't so damned rich."

The voice paused then came again, more distant now.

"You ought to know. If you hadn't broken your leg out there at Manykill I'd have had to kill you tonight. It wouldn't have pleasured me. Killing never has. Leastways a man like you. But I'd have done it.

"I intended to, before your accident. When the time came. So you couldn't track me. Count your blessings, Spence, and let be. You'll never have a better stroke of luck than that splinted shin . . ."

If there was more, Spencer Stanton did not hear it.

CHAPTER 15

Stanton became aware that he was gasping, reaching deep for breath. Some acrid inhalation was coursing the passages of his head and throat. Its bite stung his mind back to consciousness.

He sensed the strong, acrid, urine-scented odor of lingering snow melting on an unclean corral on a warm spring day. He opened his eyes. Doc Magruder was bent over him, passing a phial of aromatic ammonia before his nostrils. He sneezed and pushed away Doc's hand.

"For God sake, let a man breathe!" he protested.

"Amyl hydrate. Probably damn near straight fusel oil. I smelled it the minute I came in. Who slipped it to you?"

"Kinchloe."

"The hell. Why?"

"The money from the herd. Oliver delivered it

about sunset. In cash."

Magruder whistled sympathetically.

"Hardly his style, the bastard," he said. "Easier to pull a trigger. You're that lucky."

"So he said."

Stanton sat up with an effort. It was only then that he saw Tito standing at the foot of the bed. The boy's face was haggard with sleeplessness, concern, and now a stunned disbelief.

"What the hell are you doing here?" Stanton demanded.

"I know you're not going to like it, Pa, but we stopped early last night. Every last one of us just couldn't go on with you laid up alone here. We talked it over. We knew we all couldn't come back. You wouldn't stand for that. They picked me. Hugo and Raúl said I was the only one you'd let stay. They said it was my duty."

Stanton said nothing. Tito waited miserably.

"I had to obey their orders, didn't I? Like I do yours. You made them boss."

"Did *you* think it was your duty, contrary to my orders?"

"Yes, sir. I'd have come anyway, whoever they picked. I rode all night and I'm staying till we can go home together. You've got to understand, Pa. I just have to."

"Don't be stubborn, Stanton," Magruder said. "I'll write you out a prescription saying his presence is absolutely essential. In my opinion it is. Especially now."

Stanton glanced at the window. The curtain

had been drawn back. The sun was not high. Not as much time had been lost as he feared.

"Mighty early for a man with a perpetual hangover," he growled.

"Don't give me credit I haven't earned," Magruder answered. "Bobbie, here, woke me about sunup. He found you out cold and thought you'd had a relapse or something. It's taken better'n an hour to bring you around and I don't like practicing before breakfast. Sours my stomach."

"Kinch actually gave you that stuff, Pa — whatever Doctor Magruder calls it? He actually stole our money?"

"He did. Your friend. Mine. Intended to from the night he rode into our camp out there on the Arkansas west of Pawnee Crossing."

"I can't hardly believe it," Tito said slowly. "I — I liked him. I thought he liked me. And you."

"Oh, he was gentlemanly," Stanton said grimly. "Even apologized, I think. Said he was sorry or something like that. I was nearly out by then. Whatever it was flattened me like a cave-in in a cutbank."

"Does that," Magruder agreed. "I've seen customers at the Redeye that Willie's slipped the drops to go off in the middle of a hell of an argument between one fighting cuss word and the next without ever knowing what hit 'em. Ever now and then Willie overdoes it and the customer don't come back. Even with Jed Magruder in attendance. Then I don't get paid. Hazard of the profession."

"The law," Tito said, lifting his head deter-minedly. "I'll get the law. Everybody's got to know that money's ours and he can't have gotten far. Must be a marshal or something . . ."

"Was, Bobbie," Dr. Magruder said. "A whole string of 'em since I've been here. Trouble is Jack Kinchloe's been through here before and has got the last one's badge in his pocket. Or so I've heard."

"Somebody'll help. That Mr. Oliver and his friends who bought our cattle. They're impor-tant men."

Magruder shook his head.

"And alive. They intend to stay that way. Here on the river nobody gets mixed up in hunting a man like Kinchloe. Nobody in his right mind. They're just grateful when he disap-pears and hope like hell he doesn't turn up again. Anybody else's hard luck is no part of theirs."

"Damn it —" Tito burst out. He caught his fa-ther's eye. "Well — he's not going to get away with it! Out in the Territory we hunt down thieves, Doctor Magruder. No matter who they are. And we get them."

That was enough for Stanton. He threw back the quilting and dangled his legs over the edge of the bed.

"What the devil you think you're doing?" the doctor demanded, startled.

"You heard the boy, Doc," Stanton answered

quietly. "We're going after Kinchloe and our money."

"You're out of your mind!" Magruder protested incredulously. "You're a grown man. A sensible one. That river out there leads to the whole world. No telling where he'll head. If you had your whole crew and half the Army besides you'd never run him down. And if you did he'd pick the lot off one by one, right down to Bobbie, here."

"We have some pretty curly wolves in our country, too. But we get us a pelt every now and then."

"Face it, Stanton. Kinchloe's gone. So's your money. You've been through enough. Don't stretch your luck. Wait till you can travel by stage and head for home."

Stanton gingerly put his good foot down onto the floor and shifted body weight to it.

"You double-damned fool!" Magruder said hotly. "Put that other foot to floor or ground for weeks yet — the slightest weight on it by accident or otherwise — and you've lost the leg. That's a God's-truth promise."

"Fetch me my pants, son," Stanton ordered. He shot a look at Magruder. "And my gun."

Magruder threw up his hands in despair.

"All right, *all right!*" His eyes rolled supplicantly to the ceiling. "God help the faithful physician who treats a madman. You keep your ass right where it is, Stanton. See he does, boy, or you're going to have a hobbling old cripple on your hands the rest of your life.

"I'll have old Emory make up a pair of crutches. And I've got something up in my room. A notion I've been working on. I'll be back as quick as I can."

He left hurriedly, muttering to himself. Tito brought Stanton his clothes. Together, careful of the injured leg, they got them on except that there was no way to get a boot on over the bandaged and splinted ankle. Stanton remained seated on the edge of the bed. Tito eagerly brought hot water from the kitchen. Stanton washed and shaved and felt much better for it.

Magruder returned shortly. He had a U-shaped piece of stirrup iron. The strap bar at the top had been cut out. The side straps had been flattened farther and bent inward a little. A vertical row of screw holes had been drilled in each.

"I don't know about this," Magruder said. "Never heard of anything like it ever being tried before. But I never seen splints that fit as snug and straight as those that Dutchman at Manykill carved for you either. Get that pant leg up and stretch that leg out where I can work on it without the damned thing falling off."

Magruder knelt on the floor beside the bed and began to unwrap the outer binding over the splints. He spoke over his shoulder to Tito.

"Fetch me my bag, then watch me close. It'll be up to you from now on. Once a day's enough if this outer binding doesn't loosen up. Its got to be kept snug enough to hold the edges of the splints tightly together at all times. Understand?"

"Yes, sir," Tito agreed earnestly.

The splints came away. The inner bandage was removed. Stanton saw with relief that the wound over the break was continuing to heal rapidly. It was still a damned poor excuse for a leg but it was getting there.

The doctor patiently showed Tito how to pack the injury with a carbolated salve and apply a fresh inner bandage. He let the boy do much of it himself. Tito's lips were compressed and he frowned in concentration but Stanton was pleased to see his hands were steady and sure. The job was neatly done.

Magruder took up the two halves of the splint. He fitted the altered stirrup iron to them, one side strap to each, thus fastening them together at their lower extremities with space for Stanton's foot between. Satisfied his measurements had been sufficiently accurate, he took forceps from his bag and firmly lagged the iron to the outside of the splints with small, stout cabinetmaker's screws.

Separating the splints at the top against the spring of the metal at the bottom, he carefully slipped them over the injured leg so that the joining stirrup iron passed under Stanton's foot a couple of inches ahead of the heel but extending an equal distance beyond the flesh of his sole. He then wound fresh binding over the splints from knee to ankle.

A knock sounded. Tito opened the door. An old man in a leather carpenter's apron stood there with a pair of crude but stout peeled alder crutches in one hand and a saw in the other. Magruder waved him in.

"Measure him for size, Emory. On your foot, Stanton. *Foot,* not feet. Don't let the bad one touch the floor."

With Magruder and Tito steadying him, Stanton cautiously stood erect on his good foot. After days on his back the sensation was welcome but he found he was a little light-headed.

The old carpenter placed the armrests of the crutches under Stanton's armpits. He eased his weight onto them and found the height of the horizontal hand-bars jutting from the main shaft of each at a comfortable height, but the old man did not seem satisfied and took the crutches back.

He placed them across a chair seat and cut an inch or so from the lower tips. Stanton tried them again and found he could balance more easily. But he did not like it that he had to hunch forward a little to use them effectively. He said so.

"Vanity," Magruder answered. "Emory's got a great eye for height." He turned to the carpenter. "Thanks, my friend. They'll do first-rate. If I can teach this stubborn bastard how to use them. I'll settle up later."

The old man nodded satisfaction, took up his

saw, and left. Spencer Stanton, *patrón* of the Corona, stood there on one good leg and two makeshift wooden ones, feeling unsteady, clumsy, and foolish.

"Mind me now," Magruder said. "You can't trust crutches, no matter how long you use 'em. They'll skid out from you every which way every chance they get. Or you don't swing 'em high enough over an obstacle that doesn't even stick up an inch. Down you go, off balance and harder'n hell."

"I'll manage. Man can learn anything if he has to."

"Not them," the doctor corrected. "Physical reflexes in a big, powerful man like you are faster than his brain. No offense intended. If you lose your balance, start to fall, you're going to catch yourself any way you can. Before you can think. Even with your bad leg. And if that foot hits the ground or the floor or a walk with any weight on it at all, it's really going to bust all to hell with no fixing it this time."

"Damn it, I can't go after a man with a wheelbarrow strapped to my tail and somebody trundling me at a dogtrot where I want to go."

"No. But the way it's rigged now I'm hoping your foot won't hit the ground. That stirrup iron under it will. If it works right it'll carry the shock to those splints. The snug way that Dutchman carved them, they should carry it right past the break to your upper calf and the swell under the knee with no strain on the broken bone. Not as

197

much anyway. Try a little weight on it now. Easy."

Stanton obeyed, slowly dividing the weight of his body between his good foot and the stirrup iron under the other until the crutches came free under his arms. The foot of the bad leg dangled free of the floor and the U of the stirrup iron curving under it from the lower end of one splint to the other. He could feel the pressure on the upper part of his calf and the base of his knee. There was no twinge in the broken lower shin.

"How's it feel?" Magruder asked anxiously.

"Nothing," Stanton said. "Maybe like wearing a peg leg. Sort of dead. But I'd sure hate to walk very far on it."

"You're not to try," Magruder warned sharply. "Not one step. Not even to the slop jar at night. It's for emergency only. A stumble or a fall. For God sake don't ask anything more of it, man! Not till you've given up this fool notion of yours and have been home a month. I want a promise on that."

"No promise," Stanton answered. "But you've done wonders, Doc. I'm beholden. We both are."

"And I'm as big a fool as you are."

Magruder handed Tito a tin of salve and a thick roll of hand torn muslin bandaging. He put on his coat and closed his bag.

"One thing you can't do is ride a horse. I'll see if I can find you some kind of a light rig. Maybe a good, fast buggy. You just wouldn't believe the outfits some idiots get to the river with. They think the National Road runs clean to Texas and the mountains with covered bridges and stone culverts and a smooth surface the whole damned way. They come cheap when they can be had."

Stanton leaned again into his crutches and walked to the door with the doctor, the knee of his bad leg bent to swing that foot clear of the floor.

"No need," he said as they moved. "You've done enough. We'll do on our own. It's our way."

Magruder shrugged and turned at the door.

"Next year, Stanton?" he asked.

"*Si Dios quiere,* as they say in our country."

"Until then."

They shook hands. Magruder went out, head wagging in bafflement. Stanton closed the door and swung awkwardly across the room to the drawer in which his gun lay. Tito's was atop it. He lifted out the lighter weapon and its accouterments.

"Here," he said. "Catch."

Tito caught the belt-wrapped bundle. The butt of the gun landed solidly in his palm. His finger was in the trigger guard. The barrel was half-drawn from the holster. A quick smile lighted his face. He waited for Stanton to reach out his own belt. They buckled them on together, facing each other.

"What's first, Pa?"

"We need some pocket money to bail out of here. There's a banker lives on the next floor up. Name is Kemmerer. Ask where he can be found."

199

"How much we need?"

"Enough to find John Kinchloe."

"This do it?"

Tito emptied a pocket onto the bureau. Its contents made a fair stack of gold coin.

"What Hugo and Amelio had left out of what you gave them to outfit. They thought I might need it if I ran into problems on the way back here."

Stanton eyed the heap.

"We'll make it do," he said. "Sell your horse and saddle for what you can get. The rifles, too. We won't need them on this hunt."

CHAPTER 16

It was a short block to the riverfront, no more than a dozen rods or so. Stanton was unencumbered except by his crutches, splints, and his own body. Tito lugged the new portmanteau in which they had stowed their remaining personal gear. Nevertheless, Stanton was winded and acutely uncomfortable when they reached the Leavenworth wharf. He knew Doc Magruder was right. This was folly. He rebelled at his own limitations.

Nevertheless, a worthless scoundrel and a faithless wife had once stolen hugely from him and driven him from his Virginia plantation in disgrace. He had sworn then that no one would ever again lay hand to what was his. He swore so now. He found a packing case and sank gratefully upon it to let the curious come to him since he could not seek them out.

They were not long in showing up. Two heavily muscled wharf-handlers drifted over casually, sizing him up in hope of profit. A crippled man and a boy. Well-dressed. Quality folk. Stanton saw the sense of promise in their eyes. One touched his waterman's cap in token deference.

"Be you looking for someone or somethin', Cap'n?" he asked.

"I am," Stanton agreed. "The fastest way to St. Louis. For the two of us."

He opened his hand, palm up. Two of the small hoard of gold coins Tito had salvaged lay in it. The wharfmen's interest sharpened avariciously. Stanton closed his hand again.

"That'd be the river, Cap'n," the spokesman said. "She's a long old haul overland. No downriver stage and you can't set saddle."

"No."

"Steamer'd be your style, I reckon. But you're a mite late if you're in a hurry. Downriver packet called last night. Lay to an hour and shoved off about ten. Two weeks till another."

"Unfortunate." Stanton showed the two coins again. "There's a man somewhat known hereabout. A drifter. Fancied up some of a sudden. White hat, two guns, a brand-new carpetbag. He board her?"

The two wharfmen looked at each other. The silent one nodded uneasy assent to his companion.

"He did," the spokesman answered Stanton.

"First-class cabin, port side forward." He hesitated. "You got business with Jack Kinchloe?"

"About a hundred thousand dollars worth," Stanton agreed. "Or his life. The choice is his. When we catch up with him."

The wharfman rubbed his stubbled chin.

"Well, there's a scatterin' of private downriver freightin' traffic. Like the *Owanico*, yonder. She's a keelboat. Cap Sissoon'll take passengers. There's bunks aboard and a cook of sorts for all she's a pole barge.

"Keelboats make tolerable good time, comparin, workin' upriver. They got big crews to man the poles and they cut the current cleaner. But goin' down they drink their way and drift with the current. Got to keep to the middle of the channel, too, account they draw so deep. Can't risk runnin' the faster water over the shoals and through the slots. Wouldn't gain nothin' on that steam-packet takin' *Owanico*. Kinchloe'd be in St. Louie four-five days ahead of you, best you could hope."

"Too long," Stanton said.

"So I figured," the wharfman admitted. "That leaves Scarlatine. He's had a flatboat of furs from the Mandan villages pulled in on the mudflats since daybreak, caulkin' a leak. Ought to be about ready to push off again."

"How do I get word to him?"

"We could take you down in the skiff so's you could talk to him, Cap'n. I doubt he's fit company for the boy or you, either one. But the flatboats he builds up there really go when they got water behind 'em. And he knows the chutes like no man on the river. If anybody can gain any time on that packet, it'd be him."

Stanton dropped the coins in his hand back into his pocket and lifted himself with his crutches.

"Let's go."

Scarlatine proved to be a formidable man of French and Indian ancestry. He was lithe and powerful. His evil, saturnine face was marred by a large, flaming-red birthmark which had doubtless given him the name he used. He was waist deep overside in the shallows of a backwater mudflat, driving strips of rawhide with the hair still attached into a planking seam with a crude caulking mallet.

His crew was helping, straining to career his clumsy-looking craft enough to keep the leaky seam exposed. One was another mixed breed whose antecedents Stanton could not guess. The other was a quite young, well-modeled Indian girl with a very pretty face.

All were plastered with the muck of the bottom which their efforts had stirred to the surface. All three were bare-chested and wore only makeshift breechclouts torn in strips from worn blanketing.

The flatboat was just that, a shallow, rectangular hull of rough whipsawed planking. It was square at both ends with an undershot angle of forty-five degrees from the overhang at deck level to the water and presumably to the bottom planking. Stanton thought it drew no more than eighteen inches. She was decked over so that any water that came aboard would run off without swamping her.

A makeshift, shacklike cabin, so low it could only be entered in a deep crouch or on hands and knees, sat well aft on the deck. On each side of this and forward nearly to the square bow, the cargo was stacked to roof level, leaving only a narrow walkway between cargo and gunwales.

The cargo consisted of hide-wrapped bales of raw-stretched furs of all varieties, stacked like cordwood and lashed in place. There were a lot of them, each about as much as a strong man would care to heft. Stanton supposed they repre-sented considerable value even in their stiff, bone-dry, raw state.

Scarlatine waded to the skiff and gripped the gunwale, careless that water slopped in on its passengers. He heard out the spokesman of the wharf handlers and looked Stanton and Tito over with insolent scorn, taking in the crutches and Stanton's splinted leg.

"You'd be no good to me or Godalmighty on the water," he growled. "Damned swells. Not a yard of gut in a dozen like you. A cripple and a kid at that."

"My friend," Stanton said quietly. "I can't abide a big mouth. The more so from trash like you."

The man in the water did not seem offended. To the contrary, his interest heightened.

"Trash now! Me? Scarlatine?" He laughed. "With notions like that you won't last long on *this* river, mister!"

"Have so far."

Scarlatine eyed the crutches and splint again.

"Yeah. So I see. Can you use those guns or are they just to impress the ladies with? Both of you."

Stanton saw an empty whiskey bottle with the upper third bobbing vertically above the surface of the backwater a respectable distance away. He pointed to it.

"Show him, son."

In a restricted position and at an awkward angle, Tito drew and fired so swiftly that Scarlatine flinched instinctively. The bottle exploded and vanished. The smoke drifted away. The boatman drew a long breath.

"At least the banty's got spurs," he said to Stanton. "If you can do as well. I don't haul no payin' passengers. More fault than they're worth. My profit's in my furs and I settle for that. But them that can do for themselves and work their way or earn it otherwise is welcome from here on downriver."

"We'll do what we can."

Scarlatine nodded.

"I'll take your word. You're just in time. We're finished here. Shinny aboard. Be with you directly."

He freed the gunwale of the skiff and the wharfmen put it alongside the flatboat. Tito held tight to the larger craft while the wharfmen helped Stanton heave himself onto the deck above. Tito followed with the crutches and portmanteau.

Stanton gingerly got the crutches under him and lifted himself erect, carefully shifting balance to compensate for the unfamiliar instability of the planking on which he stood. When he thought he had caught the knack, he freed one hand and retrieved the two offered gold pieces from his pocket.

"Much obliged," he told the two men in the skiff.

He flicked one coin and then the other overside with his thumb. Both were deftly caught and pocketed. The spokesman of the pair touched his knit riverman's cap with no more real deference than before.

"I wouldn't be in yours or the boy's boots for ten of those, Cap'n," he said with a wolfish grin. "Good luck to you. But don't say we didn't warn you."

His partner dipped his oars and they rowed back toward the Leavenworth wharf.

Scarlatine, the other breed, and the Indian girl had splashed a few yards away and were sloshing the muck from their bodies and hair in cleaner and more settled water. Stanton watched them porpoising like animals. Tito rummaged in the low deckhouse and returned with a small box.

He set this against the rear wall of the deckhouse. Stanton lowered himself gratefully onto it and tucked his crutches out of the way behind it against need. Tito leaned against the shaft of the great sweep oar which served as a tiller.

"How come you knew Kinch'd take to the river, Pa?" he asked. "It's a sight easier trail to follow than a careful man'd leave on a horse. And I'm not so sure it's faster traveling."

"You're saddle-bred's what makes you think so, son. Don't get it wrong. Won't be anything easy about this. You'll see."

"But how'd you know?"

"The new outfit he had on when he showed up with Oliver. Real dandied. The rich man. Quality, according to his lights. All set for the posh life. I should have known what he intended to do, right then. I'm not proud of that."

"How could you, when you trusted him? At least I did."

"I'm older. Time teaches. You should never stop learning. If you do, if you forget or don't listen to your instincts, you'll get caught between a rock and a hard place every time. Like we are now. Keep it in mind."

Tito nodded, his brow still knit in thought.

"I'm trying to," he said earnestly. "Those steam packets stop near every place on the river there's a landing, don't they? Like Leavenworth and the fort on upriver?"

"Where there's freight and passengers anyway.

They use a semaphore in daylight and a lantern at night to flag them down."

"I was just thinking. There's got to be a lot of 'em between here and St. Louis."

"Couple dozen, anyway."

"Well, I know Kinch, even if he did fool me. He's smart. He'd slip off that packet at one of them. At night, maybe, so nobody'd see him. He'd hole up there for a spell. In case we set somebody on his trail. When it cooled off he'd move on. Not before. You said St. Louis is a big town. Bigger than Sante Fe."

"Much," Stanton agreed. "Ten times. Genuine city. Queen of the west. Capitol of the fur trade. Always will be. Long as the trade lasts."

"Kinch wouldn't go there right off, then. Too many people to see him. And if they did, they'd remember him. He's that kind of a man. And sharp enough to know it. I'm afraid we'll pass him by somewhere along and not even know it."

"That's what you'd do in the same circumstances," Stanton agreed. "And you'd be right. You'd disappear. You'd get away clean. Nobody'd be able to trail you. Because you thought that way."

"Then maybe I'm right?"

"No. You can't think like yourself on a hunt, son. Not even when you're after meat in the mountains. You know that. You've got to think like a pronghorn or a whitetail or an elk or you're going to have a mighty long ride for nothing. Same when you're hunting a man. You've got to think like the one you're after."

"Like Kinch?"

"I know you were trying, but you missed him a mile. You've never wanted for anything. None of us have on the Corona in your time. But whatever he's been, wherever he's gone, Kinchloe's had nothing more often than not and little more than that in the best of times.

"That's why he's made a mistake in his thinking. He's sure I wouldn't follow him — couldn't, in fact — and he didn't figure on your coming back. He'll go to the biggest, richest city he can reach in a hurry. He'll take the best room in the best hotel, order the fanciest dinner the kitchen can turn out, and find him the prettiest woman. He'll have everything he's never had before and that money'll burn a hole in his belly till he does. Don't worry. He'll be in St. Louis and we'll find him."

Scarlatine was the first to return to the flatboat. He came jetting up out of the water in a single surge, hoisted to the deck by powerful arms and shoulders. The rag of his discarded breechclout hung about his neck. His smooth, almost hairless body was otherwise naked. He flung the dripping clout to the deck to dry where it fell, without concern for his appearance.

In a moment he reappeared with a pair of pants raggedly torn off at the knees. He stepped into them and buttoned up. Out of practicality rather than modesty, Stanton was sure. The sun was hot in the sky and glinted up savagely from the surface of the water as well. A man's unexposed skin burned readily in such light.

There was a great splashing and giggling alongside and the Indian girl sailed up over the gunwale, heaved so mightily from below that she landed gracefully on her feet on deck. She wore no more than Scarlatine had when he came aboard. Glistening with river drip, her coppery young body was magnificent. She smiled provocatively at him as she stepped past Stanton to the deckhouse cuddy. He felt the impact.

So, he saw, did Tito. The realization startled him. He remembered 'Mana's predeparture warning and briefly felt a twinge of guilt. Maybe there were some things a boy could learn too soon and too fast. But there was no help for it now.

Scarlatine, too, noted the slack-jawed expression on Tito's face as the stooping girl's buttocks disappeared within the deckhouse. He laughed.

"Some things are pretty and some prettier, *hein, mon petite ami?*" he asked.

The other breed came scrambling aboard, naked as well, and crawled into the deckhouse. Scarlatine dropped a hand to Tito's shoulder.

"Come. So you ride the river, we make a riverman of you. First, the anchor."

He pushed Tito forward along the walkway past the cargo-insulated deckhouse. Reaching up to the edge of the low flat roof behind him, Stanton pulled himself up, balancing on his good leg. Turning, he leaned against the cabin and looked forward over it. Scarlatine showed Tito two lines which led to the water from a single bitt forward.

"There is no iron for anchors up in the Mandan country where I build these boats," he said. "So we use rock. But the river, she moves and she is strong. It takes much rock to hold the boat against her. So much it would break the back of a strong man to lift it. *Voilà!* Why to sweat? We use many smaller rocks. Here, see for yourself."

He handed one of the lines from the bitt to Tito, leaving the other fast.

"Bring her in."

Tito began to heave on the line, hand over hand. The flatboat slowly edged forward in the slack water. Weight came on the line when it hung vertically. Tito's body stiffened with effort as he began to lift. A couple more yards of line came in and then a rock bumped aboard. Stanton judged it weighed twenty-five pounds or so, easy enough to hoist in the water, heavier in the air.

The stone was of natural shape, suitably elongated to be securely lashed into the continuing line. At intervals of about a yard or so other stones of similar size and general shape appeared, lashed to the line. Tito hoisted them aboard and stacked them behind the bitt. There were about a dozen, all told, an aggregate of three hundred pounds or more; yet Tito had brought them aboard without undue effort. The line to which they were lashed proved to be continuous, its far end being the second line fast to the bitt.

It was an ingenious arrangement, very practical, and Stanton could see it would have many interesting applications in tricky waters. He could begin to understand the respect of the Leavenworth wharf handlers for Scarlatine as a boatman.

The two forward came aft. Scarlatine thrust the shaft of the long steering sweep under Tito's arm and showed him how to lean against it one way or the other to swing the oversized oar blade at its business end from side to side in the water to control the course of the flatboat.

"Now we go, eh?" Scarlatine said to the boy. "See that clump of sedge sticking above the surface out there? Beyond is living water. When we pass it, turn downriver and hang on. You'll see how a Scarlatine flatboat can go. Ugly as a nigger witch, but with a burr under her tail — ha!"

For several minutes, Stanton had been absently aware of some kind of muted threshing about within the deck hovel against which he was leaning. Suddenly Scarlatine sensed it, too. He wheeled about and bellowed at the dark cuddy doorway.

"*Sacre bleu*, Jules, get your pimply ass out here and leave that squaw be! Wanta wear her out afore we're to St. Louis and can afford to buy us

213

a white one? Come on, you worthless bastard, pole!"

Scarlatine snaked down one of several slender, straight, twelve-foot lengths of peeled sapling lying along the deckhouse roof. Trotting forward along one walkway to the bow, he drove the un-shod end into the water to the bottom. Putting the padded end of the pole to his chest at the shoulder, he began to walk aft along the walkway, thrusting mightily against it.

The pole bowed and trembled. The flatboat picked up way under its thrust. Tito leaned against the shaft of the long sweep oar to point the square bow of the craft toward the clump of reeds that had been given him as a mark.

Unabashed and still as naked as a jaybird, the breed Scarlatine had called Jules crawled from the cuddy and retrieved his soggy blanketing clout from the deck. He wrapped this once about his waist, passed the long end between his legs up in back to tuck into the first wrap. Thus attired to his satisfaction he snaked down another of the poles from the cuddy roof and went forward along the other walkway to pole on that side.

Scarlatine pushed his pole aft again and glared at the breed in the bow.

"Sonovabitch!" he complained to Stanton. "Cheats ever chance he gets, even for one quick hump. It ain't even his day."

CHAPTER 17

The immense power of the Missouri was deceptive. It seemed tranquil in its majesty, unhurried. Yet close enough inshore to make a proper estimate, the bank rushed past with surprising speed.

The poles had been restowed as soon as they were out of slack water into the main stream. Tito took to it with delight, spending every hour Scarlatine would allow at the steering sweep. Drifting free as she was, it seemed impossible that the flatboat could move faster than the general flow of the river, yet it did. They continually overhauled and passed floating debris.

Scarlatine delighted in Tito's enthusiasm and took every occasion to show him fine points of flatboating.

"Now take the way you handled that little gun of yours," he said. "Somewhat of that you learned."

215

Tito agreed. "From Pa and some others on the grant, too. But mostly from a man I thought was my friend."

"Just some. The rest of it's in you, no? Things you never been taught because nobody can teach 'em. Things that are just there. Things you just know, you just feel. Like how to breathe. *Hein?*"

Scarlatine pointed ahead to where smooth-running water rose in a small, unfrothed, constant hump like a little wave anchored in one small place.

"See that niggerhead yonder? Steer just to miss it."

Tito leaned on the sweep and they passed the hump close aboard.

"You saw it and so knew it was there. But what at night? Did you notice anything as we came down on it?"

"Well, I'm not sure, but it seemed like the boat started to raise a little and lean away from it as we got close."

"*Trés bien!*" Scarlatine exclaimed. "Already the river is in your blood. That's the warning you get when you can't see the water. Niggerheads are the biggest danger. Snags stuck too far below the surface to break the current and show white water. Or a hard sandbar. Snags'll rip out the bottom and a bar will break the back of the best boat ever built. When you can't see 'em that's *all* the warning you get.

"A chute or slot is something else. There you can see the danger, where the best water is. Or you can hear it and the current helps you steer when you can't see. Watch . . ."

Scarlatine took the sweep from Tito and crabbed the boat across the current from the Kansas shore, which they had been following for several miles, toward the Missouri bank on the inside of a sharp turn in the constant meandering of the river. A long, narrow island appeared about a hundred and fifty yards out from the bank. Sound came and they could see white water between the island and the shore. Scarlatine steered gleefully into it.

The boat picked up speed alarmingly and the sound grew to a roar. The craft began to pitch and rock violently. Water roiled aboard forward, rushed aft to wet their feet, and cascaded overboard astern. Scarlatine grabbed Tito and thrust the shaft of the sweep oar back under his arm.

"Ride her, boy!" he cried. "Hold her straight and let her go."

Motion became more violent. Spray flew higher. Twice Tito was nearly knocked from his feet by the turbulence against the sweep. Chuckling, Scarlatine moved to Stanton and hunkered beside him.

"One season, *m'sieu*, and he'd know the Big Muddy from one end to the other. This is how we gain on a steam packet. Few stops and take the chutes wherever we can. Always the fast water."

"How far behind will we be?" Stanton asked.

"A guess. Who knows? It was twelve hours at

Leavenworth. Say six at St. Louie. With luck."

"You need it," Stanton yelled above the sound of the river. "Lose your boat and you've lost a season to build another and get her back up the river."

"All she has to do is get me down. I sell her in St. Louie along with the furs. Cash money and a pack of trade goods to take back with me. I raise a little hell, make some good fun for myself, and take a packet back up as far as she goes. Then buy a couple horses and ride the rest of the way.

"Come another season and I got enough furs to make it worthwhile, I build another boat and ride her down again. Three-four thousand profit a trip. A good business, *m'sieu*."

"What about Jules, whoever comes down with you? You take them back up?"

"No profit in that. They want to see St. Louie. *Voilà*, they see. What they do then is their affair."

"The girl who's with you now?"

"A little side deal. Jules and me make the partnership. For down the river. Company. One day with me, one with him. When we get to St. Louie we sell her."

"Sell her!"

"Her pap would do the same upriver. For horses, furs, a gun and powder. A trader makes a profit where he can." Scarlatine laughed at Stanton's disapproval. "They buy and sell niggers. What's the difference? They do not see many Indians in St. Louie these days. Young ones with big *tettes*. Valuable merchandise there."

Stanton was appalled at the callousness but supposed there was some validity to the argument and let it go. There was no appeal to men who merely aped their betters and felt justified in all things by so doing.

"Profit, since it seems so important to you. Show me profit in taking me and my boy aboard."

"We'll find out where the Osage joins the river. Somewhere along. Thieves sometimes wait there. They take the furs they steal into St. Louie and claim they came from their own traps. Every merchant knows there's no beaver left in those waters, but they ask no questions if the pelts are prime and the price is right. They know the plew was stolen but few boatmen live to complain, so nothing is said."

"Our guns, then. As guards. What we call riding shotgun on stages out in our part of the country."

"Something like, I guess. I'm no shakes with a short gun. Jules is worse. Long ones take too long to load when they're onto you. Besides, it takes the two of us to handle the boat. If they come out, you'll earn your passage. If they don't, you're my guests. I'm a generous man when it suits my convenience, *m'sieu*."

"No doubt. I also rather suspect you're a bastard."

Scarlatine laughed again.

"*Oui,* as a matter of fact, I am. For two genera-
tions, now."

The lower end of the island behind which they
had been running dropped astern. Sound dimin-
ished. They slowed into more placid water.
Scarlatine relieved Tito at the sweep. The boy's
eyes were bright with pride in meeting the challenge of the chute. The Indian girl appeared in
the deckhouse entry and beckoned to him. Tito
crossed and disappeared within. In a moment he
emerged, dragging a shallow, sand-filled firebox
out onto the deck.

The girl brought out some whittlings and
kindling and started a small, hot fire over old
charcoal. She was still barefooted but decorously
clad now in the long, straight-hanging dress of
her people. The soft, supple buckskin whispered
seductively as she moved. Tito watched her with
fascination.

Jules took over the sweep. Scarlatine produced
a used saddle of venison wrapped in a dirty piece
of canvas. He put it on the deck beside the girl
and crawled into the deckhouse. The girl unwrapped the meat, reached a knife from within
her dress at the nape of her neck, and began to
slice it.

Stanton had long since acquired a stockman's
self-regard as a connoisseur of table meat. He
had too often been obliged to eat of a fresh kill
not to recognize the improvement to be had in
tenderness and flavor by a judicious amount of

aging. The fare the girl was preparing had been far too long butchered.

The odor was overpowering. Stanton shuddered involuntarily. Tito was more obvious. He pinched his nostrils together with his fingers. The girl, however, seemed to think the meat prime and sniffed appreciatively of a strip as she skewered it with others on a rusty old ramrod. She thrust forked sticks into the sand of the firebox and placed the ramrod across them over the fire.

She had a sack of corn ears on which the husks and silk had not yet completely dried. She wet them in the river and placed them about the perimeter of the fire to steam. As the meat began to brown and crust, she turned it attentively. Scarlatine reappeared with a small glass phial of some oily, greenish-black liquid. He sank crosslegged on the deck and placed this beside him.

The girl, testing the meat with the point of her knife, finally nodded satisfaction and lifted the ramrod skewer from the fire. She offered it first to Scarlatine. He slipped off a strip with his fingers and reached for a steaming ear of corn. The next choice went to Tito with an incongruously shy smile.

He uncertainly and uncomfortably emulated his host and looked helplessly about for some hope of escape. Next was Jules. He went wolfing at his portion at once with a great smacking of lips. The last choice was Stanton's. He saw that by chance or intent his was the largest piece of the meat. He looked at it with distaste. Scarlatine saw his hesitation and grinned.

"Weak gat, *m'sieu?* Ain't you heard? They say that when maggots won't touch it is when meat's fit for rivermen. If you're going to be puny about it, I got just the thing."

He unstoppered the phial beside him.

"Buffalo gall," he said proudly. "Likely the last you'll ever see. Got it two seasons back from an Oglala who'd kilt him a stray old bull on the Belle Fourche. A drop's all I can spare, but it'll do the trick."

He held up the phial for Stanton to sniff its contents. The scent nearly brought up Stanton's stomach intact. Knowing he could not eat the meat in his fingers in its present state, he shrugged resignedly and allowed Scarlatine to tilt a single drop from the phial onto his portion.

"Bien," Scarlatine approved. "Now pop her into your mouth all at once so's she can mix as you chaw."

Closing his eyes and steeling himself, Stanton did so. To his astonishment the taste was not unpleasant. In fact there was a sharp, cleansing flavor which rendered the meat reasonably palatable. He shucked his ear of corn and mowed off three or four rows of the still flavorful kernels.

It was no banquet but it set well enough on his stomach when it was down and he was hungry. At her gestured insistence he accepted another piece of the dark venison from the girl's ramrod and another drop from Scarlatine's phial of buffalo gall.

Tito refused the Indian condiment completely and after stalling as long as he could he ate his portion of the meat as it came from the ramrod, swallowing quickly without chewing. Stanton could see his anguish but he finished the meal with manful effort.

Almost at once the fire was quenched and the firebox stowed. Jules handled the sweep with greasy hands, sucking at his fingers. Scarlatine thrust the girl before him into the deckhouse. He paused at the entry.

"We'll run most of the night. Bad water about thirty mile down. We'll anchor short of it before morning to wait for light. Thought I'd warn you in case we step on you in the dark or something."

"Thoughtful," Stanton said dryly.

Scarlatine smiled mockingly.

"Way I was brung up."

He crawled into the cuddy after the girl. Tito reached diffidently after them and dragged out the portmanteau. He broke out the two blankets they had in it and would have fetched bandaging, too, but Stanton shook his head. He would rather risk unchanged dressing than exposure of his injury to the filth of the flatboat.

Tito seemed to understand without explanation. He draped one of the blankets about Stanton and hunkered down miserably with the other about his own shoulders.

Presently Jules began to sing at the sweep. It

was a monotonous, wailing sound, the words meaningless to Stanton, but it seemed to give the breed pleasure. Under its cover Tito hunched closer.

"They always eat meat like that?" he whispered.

"When they have to, I suppose. Empty enough belly makes swallowing anything easier."

He felt Tito shiver with aversion.

"I don't think I like him, Pa. Or Jules either. Something's wrong. That girl — I think she's hardly older'n me."

"Could be," Stanton agreed bleakly. "Short life at best for some of them. They start early."

"I mean she doesn't talk. You notice? Not even in her own tongue that I can tell. Just a kind of a giggle once in a while. And I don't think she's laughing then. They haven't said anything to her either. Some kind of a signal or a look is all. Mean, too. I'm afraid for her. I think she is, too."

"Different world, son. Different people. Sometimes there's no accounting. You all right?"

"Tolerable, I guess," Tito lied.

"It'll pass. Turn in and try to get some sleep."

"How about you?"

"All right for now," Stanton lied in turn. "I can manage when I'm ready."

Tito stretched out athwart the deck where the motion of the boat would disturb him least and rolled into his blanket. Stanton noted enviously that it was only moments before he slept. There were virtues in youth for all its uncertainties. He thought the greatest was that the young could shut off the workings of their mind when fatigue demanded, whatever the problems confronting them.

Twilight left the sky. Night became a stygian blackness which swallowed the land. Time stretched out as interminably as the river and the infinite panoply of distant stars overhead. Presently Spencer Stanton himself dozed upright on his box with his bad leg stretched out before him and his back braced against the wall of the deckhouse.

Sometime later Tito started to retch violently. He scrabbled on his hands and knees to the nearest gunwale and hung his head overside, emptying himself in agonized paroxysms of nausea. Stanton knew there was nothing to be done for him that nature could not do of itself and he remembered the acute humiliation of such attacks and so remained motionless. Jules completely ignored the stricken boy.

Shortly the sobbing gasps subsided and Tito crawled back into his blanket. He soon slept again. So did Stanton. He had no idea how much more time had passed when he was roused by the sound of the anchor stones bumping overboard at the bow.

Scarlatine was now at the sweep, hair awry from sleeping. He put the long steering oar hard over. The boat slewed around and nosed into the current. It drifted backward a few yards until the makeshift kedge caught and held fast to the bottom.

Jules came back along the walkway from the anchor bitt. He and Scarlatine ran lines from the sweep to cleats on both gunwales to hold it firmly in a midships position. Satisfied that the boat would ride securely as was until daylight, both returned to the cuddy.

False dawn finally came, gray and chill. Just as the rim of the sun began to burn at the mists, the faintest of deliberate sounds drew Stanton's attention to the deckhouse entry. The Indian girl crouched there, barely visible. She held her index finger to her lips in a nervous signal for silence and glanced apprehensively behind her.

Apparently satisfied that her movement had not awakened the sleeping boatmen, she faced Stanton again. She pointed sharply at Stanton and then at Tito. Her knife appeared. She made a slashing gesture across her throat and indicated the men in the cuddy at her back.

Stanton saw that Tito had been right. She was tense, earnest, desperately frightened. He knew Indian pride and capacity for self-containment. It had taken a hell of a lot of bullying of a repulsively bestial kind to bring her to this terrorized appeal to strangers.

He understood her signal at once and nodded that he did so. There was instant relief in the girl's eyes, together with something that might have been a flicker of hope. He raised his eyebrows questioningly, pointing to the mist-hazed rim of the sun, and swiftly held up one finger, then two, then three.

The girl responded quickly with an eloquent shrug. Stanton nodded again and she vanished soundlessly. He drew a long and weary breath.

It was a clear-enough warning. She did not know when — one day, two, three — but Scarlatine did not intend that his passengers reach St. Louis. Stanton doubted he would take any action before the mouth of the Osage. Not until they had encountered the thieves reputedly working the river in that vicinity or had passed safely through. Anytime, then.

Stanton looked at Tito. The boy's face was rounded in sleep. There was no vestige of the flat-muscled planes of manhood he tried so earnestly to maintain when he was awake and in the company of others. He felt again the stab of guilt that he had brought a boy — let alone his own son — into something like this. But what was done was done and there was no help for it. Only to play it out. With Jack Kinchloe yet to come.

He remembered Father Frederico's placid answer to misfortune whenever the old priest happened to be visiting the Corona in a time of adversity: *man proposes; God disposes.* A serene-enough solution for an old man of the cloth but scant comfort to a man with a ranch to run, a land to tame, a family to raise, and an empire to build for its inheritance. A man who had to live with himself at the same time.

With the best intent there were just too

damned many mistakes along the way, however a man planned, and too damned few opportunities to correct even the smallest of them. 'Mana would hold this against him a long day.

He fished out his wallet and fingered within it, counting. Barely two hundred dollars of the coins Tito had returned to him remained.

Scarlatine could not know how little the wallet contained. It would probably make no difference if he did. He knew there were coins and they were gold. For what there was and a pair of belt guns he would kill without conscience.

Like hell, Stanton thought grimly. Like bloody hell!

CHAPTER 18

They ran the torturous shoal channel which had forced them to anchor until daylight. They rode out ten sense-numbing miles of thunderous turbulence in a shortcut Scarlatine called Whiskey Chute. Back in the main channel they passed rickety landings on both shores.

A man hailed them from one, leaping into the water and splashing out toward them to his armpits in his frantic effort to be heard. Stanton could make out the plea quite plainly.

"Hey, the boat! I got a sick child here. Terrible bad sick. Got to get her to a doctor. Heave to and take her and her ma aboard. I'll pay good. Whatever you say."

Scarlatine ignored the thin, desperate yell. Seeing that the boat intended to pass without stopping, the man changed his entreaty.

"At least stop off at Jeff City. Send word for a

doctor to get up here quick as he can. Name's Morgan. Morgan's Landing. In God's name do that much!"

Scarlatine turned his back on the hailer and held the steering sweep steady.

"River's going to hell," he said. "Damn trash. Take up a swamp if it's free. Sick because they can't feed theirselves. Gone bust because they ain't got brains enough to do anything else. Allus expecting somebody else to do for 'em. Worse than the beggars on the streets of St. Louie."

Stanton was aware that Tito's eyes were on him but he made no comment. Scarlatine also eyed him warily.

"Man stop ever time he's hailed these days he'd never get downriver. To say nothing of what kind of rotten pox or flux he'd pick up for his pains. And half of 'em'll slit your throat for whatever you got on deck the minute you toss 'em a line."

Stanton still remained silent. Scarlatine misunderstood and abandoned his whining defense.

"We'd get along, *m'sieu*," he said approvingly. "You're a hard man, and practical. You see how it is and take it at that. Sometimes it ain't easy, but that's what it takes in this country."

Again Stanton made no response for the reason there was none. He doubted there was a surer sentence of death for the unfortunate than to bring a sick or injured person — man, woman, or child — aboard this filthy craft.

Instead, he took a pad from his portmanteau

and wrote a brief note with a newfangled indelible pencil against later possible need. He folded this and put it away in his pocket without explanation.

Except at mealtimes, when she was the slavey, the Indian girl remained in the low, dank confines of the deckhouse, creeping out only to relieve herself over the side as modestly as she could behind what shelter the stacked bales of fur afforded. Both rivermen thought the effort amusing and called ribald advice which brought hot color to Tito's cheeks.

The second time this happened and Stanton made no protest, Tito flared angrily.

"Shut your damned mouths," he shouted angrily. "In front of a — a lady!"

Jules and Scarlatine laughed uproariously at the word. Tito glanced apprehensively at his father. Stanton smiled approval. Heartened, Tito stopped the girl when she would have slunk back into the cuddy.

Without words or sound, by expression and gestures which had no apparent meaning in themselves, he persuaded her to go forward with him to the bow. Tito removed his boots and they sat there side by side in the heat of the long afternoon, dangling bare feet overside into the cool, moving water.

Smiles, nods, and gestures continued in what seemed a totally adequate conversation which in time became quite unselfconscious and animated. Several times the girl's giggle came again, but she genuinely laughed now. Stanton had wondered at this ability among the young before.

Little Quelí, when a toddling infant too young to speak a recognizable word, had almost from the very first been able to communicate with her older brother and the Spanish-speaking youngsters from the little adobe ranch village which had grown up below the main house of the Corona. And the new baby the same after her.

Tito himself, fluent in Spanish as well as Stanton's Virginia English, had been able to exchange wants and even thoughts with their friend Chato long before the chief of the Utes had taught him the guttural music of his own mountain language.

In each case it was done in the same way as now. A common denominator which needed only to be discovered to be used. It seemed to be one of those special gifts of early years which once lost was gone forever.

Scarlatine and Jules watched the two forward with continued mocking amusement.

"I think that sprout of yours is comin' into stud, *m'sieu*," Scarlatine said jocularly. "Want her to learn him? She's not bad for one of the tribes. Say the word and I'll give her the sign. It's all right with me an' Jules an' she'll be willin' enough or take a beatin' for it."

"I'll tell you what I think," Stanton said quietly. "I think you'd better do what the boy told you. Shut your mouth or I'll do it for you."

The amusement faded from Scarlatine's eyes. He nodded at Jules in signal to take over the sweep. His hand dropped to the hilt of a knife in the waistband of his ragged, shortened pants.

"That's too much lip for even a fun-lovin' man like me, *m'sieu*," he said malevolently. "I reckon I'm goin' to learn you manners some."

He started forward, slowly drawing the knife. Stanton unhurriedly parted his coat, hooked out his belt gun, and fired the weapon from his lap. The ball struck the blade of Scarlatine's knife. The steel snapped. Scarlatine looked at the stub left at the hilt and flung it from him, but he quickly and carefully avoided any further agressive move. Stanton put the gun back into its holster.

"So we understand each other," he said without a change of tone. "Since I seem to be giving orders for the moment, we must be nearing Jefferson City. Put in there. I want to send a message."

Scarlatine nodded, tight-lipped but controlling himself with neck-bulging effort.

"If you can afford the lost time I reckon me an' Jules can, too," he assented with poor grace. "I meant no real quarrel, *m'sieu*. You need us and we need you and the boy. Those damned guns of yours. We ain't none of us to St. Louie yet. You aim to get there. So do we."

"Agreed. And we will. If you watch yourselves."

Scarlatine nodded and returned to the sweep.

They did not have to put in at Jefferson City. Although the lights of the Missouri capital were already up when they came abreast of the long quay, a pair of nearly grown boys were working a midstream trotline from a skiff in the twilight. They were unhooking a fair catch of mudcats as the line came aboard.

Stanton hailed them over and they came alongside. He showed them one of his remaining gold coins.

"A mess of your fish," Stanton said.

"Sure," one of the boys agreed.

Careful of the sharp horns at the head and the fin spines, he tossed eight or ten of the pan-sized cats up onto the deck.

"Something else," Stanton added. "Know a doctor ashore? A good one?"

"Best in the city. My uncle."

"Will he make an emergency call a few miles upriver? Tonight?"

"If we'll get a couple more to help us row him up."

"Good. Get this to him. Tell him it's urgent."

Stanton handed down the note he had written, accompanied by the coin. The boy's teeth flashed at the feel of the gold.

"We'll have him on his way in half an hour."

The boys shifted to a tandem position on the main thwart of the skiff, each taking an oar and putting their backs to them as they rowed straightaway for the quay.

234

Tito and the Indian girl came aft. Tito dragged the firebox from the cuddy. The girl fell to on the mudcats with her knife.

They ate, relishing the fresh fish. When the deck was cleared, the Indian girl disappeared into the cuddy for the night. Tito rolled into his blanket and slept as before on the deck. Leaving Jules at the steering sweep, Scarlatine went forward into the bow and crouched there, head low in search of silhouette as he scanned the dark river ahead.

He remained there, attention fully absorbed. In about an hour, when night shadow would begin to play tricks on too intently searching eyes, he rose stiffly and came back to exchange places with Jules. The breed remained as alertly on lookout.

No explanation was offered but Stanton understood. They were approaching the area in which the boatmen expected an attempt at piracy if there was to be any. He draped his blanket about his shoulders and under its cover quietly reloaded the spent charge in his gun, making sure the caps were in place on the other nipples of the cylinder as well.

At regular intervals Scarlatine and Jules continued to exchange places, so that the alertness and vision of whichever one was forward was not dulled. Stanton remained awake until the effort became taxing and he thought Tito had rested enough to carry him a spell. He nudged the boy gently with his good foot.

Tito came awake as a mountain man did with no movement but the opening lids of his eyes. The tempo of his breathing did not change. From a yard away he seemed still sleeping. But his senses were swiftly orienting him to any change that might have taken place while he slept. Slowly, almost imperceptibly, his head turned until he could see Stanton.

Stanton yawned silently to indicate his own weariness, showed his gun briefly, and tilted his head toward Jules, who was again taking his turn at the sweep. Stretching, rolling over as though awakening on his own, Tito sat up in his blanket and noiselessly hitched over until he could rest his back against the wall of the deckhouse beside Stanton. His gun also appeared briefly beneath his blanket in evidence he understood and was ready to take over watch.

Again Stanton was startled to realize how much Tito had learned, how much he knew, how surely he drew upon that knowledge. Whatever the distance between boy and man, he had traveled much of the way. Jules, a scant eight feet away, was completely unaware the watch had been changed.

With a confidence he had felt with few companions in his life, Stanton shifted to a more comfortable position and slept almost at once. Sometime later he wakened briefly, aware the boat was crabbing across a powerful offshore current.

"The mouth of the Osage, they say," Tito murmured. "Everything's all right. Go back to sleep. You haven't had much."

Stanton did so. It was sunup when he roused again, refreshed. Tito looked none the worse for his hitch on watch but their sleepless night had told on Jules and Scarlatine. Both were heavy-eyed and surly. The wear and tear was in part, Stanton supposed, from the stress of waiting for a menace that had not yet materialized.

He noted that Scarlatine again had a knife in the waistband of his ragged pants. He thought it had been taken from the Indian girl during the night. It did not please him that the riverman was again armed. It might be true that Scarlatine had no talent with a handgun. In fact, it probably was. But with a belt knife he would be fast and exceedingly dangerous in the enforced close quarters aboard the boat.

Both banks of the river were rankly overgrown to the flood marks of spring high water. There was no evidence of clearing or habitation on either side and no landings appeared for many miles.

The two boatmen remained tautly alert. Tito and the girl again sat in the bow, their feet in the water. Scarlatine admonished them to keep a sharp lookout downstream, particularly among the numerous small islands they passed on one side or the other.

Aside from this, there was no exchange between passengers and crew. In midafternoon they passed through an easy chute into a more settled area. The effect of these renewed signs of habitation on Jules and Scarlatine was instantaneous. Their preoccupation and tensely sullen mood vanished. Scarlatine was even jovial as he left Jules at the sweep and squatted down beside Stanton against the deckhouse.

"You've fetched us luck, *m'sieu*," he said. "And it'll cost you no powder. So you've had a free ride, after all. If any of them fur thieves was waitin' I reckon we slipped past 'em in the night or they've made 'em a recent haul and are hoorawing it up in St. Louie. No trouble now from here on in."

"You're sure?"

"Too many settlers the rest of the way. Too many eyes to see and too many ears to hear what goes on out here on the river. Too many noses in somebody else's business. Settlers is like that. Busybodies. Word travels like the wind among 'em. Outfit'd be crazy to jump anybody with them to witness."

"The blessings of civilization," Stanton said dryly.

"Something like," Scarlatine agreed. "You know, *m'sieu*, I been thinking. Speaking of thieves. That *loup-garou* you aim to come up with in St. Louie — that Kinchloe. How much did you say he lifted off of you?"

"I didn't say."

"That's right, you didn't. It was them wharf rats that rowed you out to me at Leavenworth. A hundred thousand dollars, wasn't it?"

238

"Give or take a little."

"Well, now, you and the boy and that messed-up pin of yours ain't much of a match for somebody that's all there and has got that much at stake. Seems like you could do with a little help. For a price."

"We'll manage."

"Feller like that could get hisself killed in an alley or somewheres like for say five thousand."

"No doubt," Stanton agreed. "Or less. Then the rest of it would disappear and Tito and I would be hunting you instead of Jack Kinchloe. No, thanks, Scarlatine."

The riverman came to his feet.

"Two sides to every counter, *m'sieu*. Every trader knows that. Maybe this Kinchloe'd like to know you're trailin' him and what shape you're in. Maybe he'd pay for a little help, even. You think of that."

"I have," Stanton said blandly. "And I know what to do about it — if I have to. You think of that."

Scarlatine shrugged and sauntered back to the sweep, relieving Jules there. A few words passed between them in some northern patois which Stanton did not understand. Jules started forward toward the deckhouse. Stanton drew his gun and eared back the hammer. Jules hesitated, then fell meekly back to stand with Scarlatine again. Scarlatine shrugged philosophically and smiled.

Satisfied his point had been made, Stanton let

down the hammer of his weapon and reholstered it to free his hands. Reaching his crutches from behind the box upon which he sat, he lifted himself up on his good leg. As he moved, Tito called sharply from the bow.

"Scarlatine! Sandbar dead ahead!"

An instant later they struck the obstacle, hard. Without his crutches fully under him, Stanton ricocheted from the wall of the deckhouse and sprawled awkwardly along the deck. As he tried to get his knees under him, Tito and the girl came running aft along the walkway. Tito grabbed Stanton's arm to help him up but Scarlatine bawled at him.

"Take the sweep, boy! Quick, before we broach and swamp! We'll try to pole her off."

Tito ran to the steering oar to try to hold the stern into the current. Scarlatine and Jules scrambled for the poles on the deckhouse roof. The Indian girl slid a crutch into Stanton's reach. He dragged it clumsily to him and started to get up again. Scarlatine and Jules seized their poles. The Indian girl cried out in a curious, inarticulate sound which seemed torn from her.

It was only then, when he was using his hands to support himself with the crutch and he could not reach his gun, that Stanton understood the weapons the boatmen had elected to use. Weapons at which Scarlatine at least was a master. Holding his pole horizontal across his chest, both hands gripping it at midlength, Scarlatine spun powerfully.

The two ends of the pole swung like brutal, blunt scythes. One struck Tito at the belt while he yet clung to the steering sweep. The force of the blow knocked the wind from him, broke his grip on the big oar, and drove him overside into the current boiling past the grounded boat.

The other end of the pole dipped for Stanton's head as it swung swiftly. He dropped again to the deck, but it would have smashed his skull had not the Indian girl leaped like a human projectile at Scarlatine, staggering him and causing the sweeping pole to lift at the last moment of its swing. Even then it sent Stanton's hat flying.

Rolling frantically onto his back, Stanton cleared his gun. Scarlatine had already reversed the swing of his pole and it was slashing back. Stanton shot him under the chin and at such short range the ball tore out the back of his head. He sprawled overboard without bloodying the deck.

Scarlatine's swinging pole, dropped from nerveless hands while still in motion, glanced from the deck of its own momentum and slammed into Stanton's shoulder with numbing force. His gun slid from momentarily paralyzed fingers and skittered across the deck. Hooking frantically with his good leg, he caught the spinning weapon with his toe before it reached the scuppers and raked it back to him, fumbling it up with his other hand.

The Indian girl, in a desperate attempt to reach the side and leap overboard, had ducked inside the sweep of Jules' pole, too close for it to be effective against her. Letting the pole clatter unheeded to the deck, Jules seized her by the throat, crushing it in the furious clamp of both knotted hands as he jerked her around bodily to screen him from Stanton.

Flat on his back, awkwardly lining his gun overhead and almost within stomping distance, Stanton put a ball through one of the breed's exposed, wide-spraddled legs at the ankle. The shot brought him down but he pulled the girl down with him, his double grip on her throat unbroken and tightening savagely in agony.

Heaving himself forward, dragging his bad leg, Stanton brought the barrel of his gun down across the clamping wrists. He heard bone snap. The girl spun free, leaped to her feet, and plunged overside into the river. With the girl clear, Stanton shot Jules again in the ribs a handbreadth above his navel. The range was so close the flesh blackened about the point of entry.

Stanton rolled over and dragged himself to the gunwale over which the girl had disappeared. Tito lay in the water, washed up against the sandbar upon which Scarlatine had deliberately run them. The girl splashed to him, seized his hair to lift his face above water, and dragged him a little higher on the sand.

Dropping to her knees in the wash beside him, she put her mouth to his and blew his collapsed lungs full of air. Tito took two deep breaths on his own, thrust her back, and sat up. He belched up a gout of water, then realized his gun was missing. Stumbling to his knees, he began feeling desperately beneath the surface for it. It was the girl who found the weapon where it had spilled when the current rolled his body against the bar.

With the sweep oar unattended, the stern of the flatboat was swinging around with the current and the movement sucked the blunt bow from the grip of the sand. Tito and the girl thrust hard, helping, until the boat floated free and the bottom dropped from under their feet. They hoisted themselves aboard and sprawled on the deck near Stanton to regain their wind.

Sidewise to the current, the boat struck another small obstacle and careened briefly. Jules' limp body rolled down the canted deck. No one made any move to stop it and it spilled overboard to become another piece of flotsam floating down the river.

Stanton was the first to regain his composure. He crawled to his crutches, awkwardly hoisted himself to his feet, and returned to his usual box against the deckhouse. Tito rolled over on his back and looked up at him.

"I was right about them, wasn't I? That was deliberate. They meant to kill us."

Stanton nodded.

"For our guns and the gold in our pockets. Maybe a chance at Kinchloe and what he's got in his carpetbag later — if they could find him and figured the odds were right. I was expecting it." Stanton indicated the Indian girl. "She warned me. Just didn't know exactly when or how. Like to have had us on account of that."

"You could have told me."

"Enough for you to do. Like trying to get us ashore at the first landing you spot."

"We can't make this kind of time ashore. How about putting us in at St. Louis?"

"Think you can?"

"I had a good teacher."

"You're the captain. Give me your gun. I'll see what I can do for it after that bath."

CHAPTER 19

Tito proved to be a good pilot, even in the great eddies swirling where the brown Missouri stained the gray bosom of the Mississippi with her silted blood. He put them ashore at the long stone quay fronting the imposing Pratte Mercantile Company warehouse.

With no other recourse, Stanton sent him ashore to find someone willing and capable to assume responsibility for the Indian girl and suggesting a church as the likeliest source of assistance or information.

They lay in the heart of St. Louis with the tumult of the city about them. The girl was round-eyed and uncomprehending, stunned by the traffic afloat and ashore and uneasy at Tito's departure. Her shoulders were rounded inward with a fear she did not understand and she huddled close to Stanton where he sat on his box against the flatboat deckhouse.

Passersby noted the baled furs with which the craft was laden. Some showed ill-concealed and lively interest. However, Stanton's gun lay across his lap and none accosted them.

It was nearly two hours before Tito reappeared. He was accompanied by an improbable figure of a man. He was a good span taller than Stanton and outweighed him by fifty pounds or more. The crown of his head was bald and as ruddy as polished maple. It was surrounded by a luxuriant fringe of curly, flaming red hair. He was barefooted and his vast bulk was draped in a great, black tent of a cassock, belted at the ample middle with a length of rope and its hem sweeping the cobblestones.

His name was Fray Robusto, Tito said as he introduced them. He had been directed to him at the Gospel Mission, farther down the waterfront. Despite this identification and the beaded crucifix dangling against his great chest, Stanton doubted this was an ordained priest, at least as humble men of the cloth were known and revered in the mountains of New Mexico. But there was an outgoing openness about him and a warm and humorous kindness in his eyes which inspired confidence in spite of doubt.

The huge friar had little interest in Stanton or his explanations and cut them short. His concern was for the girl. He spoke to her gently in several dialects, one after another, using them fluently. She displayed only puzzlement and total lack of comprehension.

Suddenly the big man fell silent and his fingers began to speak for him. So did his hands and arms and face and parts of his body. The swift gestures and finger forms moved nearly as fast as the eye. The girl brightened immediately, hopefully, eagerly answering in kind.

"Ah, there's the rub!" Fray Robusto said. "Poor wee one. She has no gift of speech. Some affliction of childhood, I think. Wait, now; we'll see."

His flying fingers resumed conversation with the girl. With no grasp of meaning, Stanton could see the run of her emotions in her quick responses: fright, sorrow, anguish, suffering, terror, and now a great flooding of relief and gratitude.

"Her name — how do you say such a name in a European tongue?" the friar said. "Bright Water will have to do, though it's lovelier than that. She's a Hidatsa, from the forks of the Missouri. Her father's an important man in that part of the country."

Fray Robusto paused and studied Stanton sharply.

"She was stolen by two men," he continued. "On a boat. This boat. You and the boy? No. Impossible. I can see that. Two evil men who used her as they would a latrine, the whole way down the river. Until you came aboard. Where was that — St. Joe, Westport, Independence?"

"Leavenworth," Stanton answered. "Murderous bastards. They tried to kill us all a day upriver."

"Yes. So she says. You saved her life."

"The other way around. She saved ours. Or did her best to. It cost them theirs."

"The furs — the boat — you're claiming them?"

"We are," Stanton agreed. "For her. If she can be taken care of. Sent safely back where she came from, if that's what she wants. Granting boat and cargo can be legally sold."

"My friend, I am a modest man, as you can plainly see," the friar said. "Have no fear for the little one. I have a few friends in St. Louis. More on the river. Whoever I protect is safe. Whatever I sell is legally sold if I say so. I am known to dislike argument in matters of business."

"That I believe," Stanton said with a smile. "You will take care of it then? And her? We have urgent business here but my son and I are unwilling to take it up until we're sure she's in good hands."

Fray Robusto held up his hamlike fists, flexing the fingers.

"I think these will do. There are Sisters in charge at the mission. We boast a civilization of sorts here but too often still young ones from the tribes are brought in for the bordellos. We rescue all we can. The Sisters will watch over her until I can find a suitable way to send her back upriver to her family. With the dowry you have provided."

"Scarlatine," Stanton corrected. "He and his

248

half-breed deckhand owed her that much at least."

"The *padre* saw Kinch and knows where he is, too," Tito said.

"Brother, boyo, not *padre*," the friar protested genially. "The good priests of the city would vomit at their devotions if they thought me ordained. Robusto may have the progeny but not the virtues of a father, I fear."

He turned to Stanton.

"The man you seek checked directly into the Sans Souci when he landed. A bawdy palace masquerading as an elegant hotel. Actually the most notable house of worldly pleasures north of New Orleans."

"Remarkable you spotted him so readily."

"Perhaps a kinship of nature."

"He's still alone?"

"A man who spends as he does is never alone. Even as a stranger in a strange city. Not while his money lasts. This one has made many eager friends in the half day since he arrived. Does he suspect you have followed him?"

"No. He can't possibly have an inkling."

"It will be difficult to reach him, even so. You will go to the law?"

"Would you?"

"No. Not here. Not when he has the money and you have none, as your boy says. I'd take my chances with luck and a prayer. But crippled up, I don't know."

"Neither do I," Stanton admitted. "Guess

there's only one way to find out."

"I'll consign this boat and cargo to the Pratte company to sell for the little one. They'll send men to unload. And you'll want a carriage with that leg. I wish I could do more. I have the appetite for it. But the nature of my vows . . . you understand."

"Perfectly," Stanton agreed. "We're beholden."

Fray Robusto spoke to the girl again with his hands. She nodded and went to Tito. She gripped his upper arms with small hands, kneading the flesh there for a moment. There was no more of a farewell than that, but it was strangely poignant.

She turned and stepped to the quay. Fray Robusto took her arm. They crossed the quay and disappeared into the cavernous interior of the Pratte company warehouse. Almost immediately roustabouts emerged and boarded the boat to commence unloading. They helped Stanton and Tito ashore with their portmanteau. A carriage rounded the corner of the big warehouse and clattered down the cobbles to them. Stanton hoisted himself into it. Tito settled beside him.

"The Sans Souci," Stanton told the driver. "There's a discreet entrance to the hotel section?"

"How discreet, boss?" the man asked with a grin.

Stanton found one of his remaining gold

pieces and dropped it into the shamelessly waiting palm.

"About so," he said.

The driver appraised the coin and dropped it into his pocket.

"For that even the head clerk won't know you're registered, Captain," the driver said.

He shook out his reins and they climbed a steep street toward the bluffs and the great houses of the city.

They entered the Sans Souci through a small vestibule off an alley at the rear. A deferential, expensively uniformed porter escorted them down a narrow rear hallway to a simple, un-marked door which let them into the most sump-tuous quarters Stanton believed he had ever seen. Tito, accustomed to the huge but simply furnished rooms of the Corona house, was vastly impressed.

Acutely conscious of body sweat, the stink of the river, and the accumulated grime of travel, the boy avoided the elegant upholstery and sat diffidently on the only simple wooden chair in the extensive parlor. Seemingly without direc-tion, servants appeared. A tray was set on a side table with fine crystalware, a stately bottle of Roanoke's finest whiskey, and a stone jug of sar-saparilla for Tito.

By the time Stanton had poured and savored a drink, baths were ready in the adjoining bed-rooms. The portmanteau was unpacked, and, as they shed the clothes they had been wearing, all items that needed attention were whisked away. By letting his splinted leg hang over the edge at the knee, Stanton managed his tub without difficulty, relishing the luxury of the bath with sensual enjoyment.

Tito came in, self-consciously wrapped in the towel-like dressing gown the house had provided for each and set about the too-long-delayed task of changing the dressing on Stanton's leg. When the splint was removed and the inner bandaging lifted away, they found the wound clean and healing well. Tito redressed it with unguent and fresh bandaging.

As he started to replace the splint with its stirrup-iron reinforcement under the instep, Stanton cautioned him.

"Fit it as snug as you can," he said. "And wrap that outer bandage as tight and smooth as you can make it. I'm going to have enough on my mind tonight without worrying about it working loose at the wrong time."

Tito nodded earnestly.

"I've been wondering what's the best way."

"So have I, son. I think I've got it worked out. The best we can do under the circumstances anyway."

"Wait till we can catch him in his room, I suppose," Tito said thoughtfully. "Maybe bribe one of the servants to find out so we can be sure. He's bound to have the money with him. He wouldn't trust anybody else with it. Jump him suddenly.

The two of us and him alone, we'll have the best chance catching him by surprise."

"No," Stanton said. "In the first place, he won't have the money with him. Not all of it. He's no fool. Just enough to cover his pleasures temporarily. A bank's my guess. Their vault. Word he's rich wouldn't have gotten around so fast, otherwise. And it'd be safe there."

Tito shook his head, frowning worriedly.

"Going to be awfully hard for us to get our hands on it if we have to kill him, and knowing him we probably will. No way to prove it's ours when he's the one that put it in the bank."

"I don't intend to kill him unless I have to. And I don't intend to jump him in his room. For one thing, a man like that's the worst kind to take by surprise. He's too fast. He'll shoot before he thinks. And I don't intend to go back to the Corona in a box.

"For another, when he goes to his room, he won't be alone. He'll have a woman or I miss my guess. A witness. The worst kind of a witness there is because money's what she'll be after, too. And she'll lie to all hell if she thinks there's a chance she can get her hands on some of it — any of it."

"I don't see how we can get to him without any witnesses."

"We want witnesses. A lot, not just one. All we can get. To hear what's actually said. To see what actually happens. So we're going to call on Mister Kinchloe at dinner. Before dessert. In

253

front of half of the important people in St. Louis if your friend the friar was right about the class of trade the public rooms in this place serve."

"He may have friends with him then," Tito objected. "Fray Robusto said he'd already made some."

"Not friends," Stanton corrected. "He hasn't had time. Or the inclination, I think. Hangers-on, kowtowing for a free ride on the money he's spending. They'll scatter fast enough at a showdown. Unless one or two see a chance for a cinch pat stand. We'll damned well make sure they don't get that."

Tito finished wrapping Stanton's splinted leg, taking great care the outer binding was as tight and snug as he could make it. They went to their separate rooms off the parlor of the suite and sprawled on their beds to make up for some of the sleepless hours aboard the flatboat. Tito dropped off at once. Stanton could hear his heavy, untroubled breathing. Stanton's body rested obediently enough but he could not sleep.

Too much that was chancy and uncertain lay ahead. Too much which had to be staged precisely and carried out without a falter. The impact of scene and timing depended wholly upon retaining control once the confrontation was put in motion. If Kinchloe succeeded for even a moment in arresting the pattern to which Stanton had committed himself in his mind — if others were allowed to intervene even momentarily, either by intent or an accident of surprise — the

Corona would have lost.

In such case, the result was a foregone conclusion. Spencer Stanton would have lost his life, perhaps gravely endangering Tito's as well. He had no illusions on this score. He knew the odds and his own limitations too well to cling to false hopes. So he lay there, going over it meticulously in his mind again and again as a skilled actor would rehearse a part, so action would be automatic, instinctive, and his mind would be clear to deal only with John Kinchloe and his reactions.

About six their clothing was returned, both that from their backs and the contents of their portmanteau. Boots were burnished to high polish. Linen was laundered to snowy white and starched and ironed faultlessly. Suiting was cleaned and brushed and pressed to as impeccable an appearance as though new and from the finest tailor's in the city.

Stanton insisted they dress in their best. They would still appear as outlanders to the society of St. Louis. The stamp of the mountains would remain upon them. But that was to their advantage. At least they could boast the arrogance of quality and a visual air of importance. It would to some degree offset the handicap of his crutches and splinted leg and Tito's youth.

Satisfied with their appearance, Stanton strapped on his gun. Tito started to do the same. Stanton shook his head.

"Not tonight," he said. "You won't be needing it. Leave it here."

"Not tonight!" Tito protested incredulously. "It's the only time I've ever really needed it since you gave it to me. The first time you've really needed me except when you were sick."

"Just the same, not tonight," Stanton repeated firmly.

"You won't have a chance with those crutches and your leg," Tito urged. "For the first time I can do something. I can help. As much as any man. Don't you trust me?"

"Completely. But I don't trust Kinchloe. He knows the easiest way to shake me is through you. But without the gun you're a boy, my son, and I think that's the way he'll treat you. I think he'll let you be. In fact, I'm counting on it and intend to see he does."

Tito started to protest further but Stanton stopped him with an upraised hand.

"You'll have your part. I promise you that. And it won't be easy. It'll take all the guts you have. But no gun. Wear it and Kinchloe'd kill you as quickly as he would me. Maybe quicker, because there'd be the two of us and he'd want to cut the odds fast. Or because he knows you'd do the same to him if you had to and had the slightest edge. If shooting starts.

"I don't intend to let it if I can help it, but you'll be taking enough risk as it is. No gun. That's final."

Stanton crossed to the bell pull and rang. The

uniformed porter responded in a few moments.

"We will be dining with Mr. John Kinchloe's party tonight," Stanton told him. "Would you let us know when he has been seated?"

Stanton took a gold piece from his vest and dropped it into the porter's hand.

"We are old friends and would prefer our arrival to be a surprise."

The porter nodded assent and departed silently. Stanton sat down to wait with a gut tightening of impatience.

Across the room, seated stiffly on a divan beside his unwillingly abandoned belt and gun, Tito continued to look at him accusingly. It was a difficult gaze to bear. His son, he saw, was desperately afraid. Not for himself but for Spencer Stanton.

CHAPTER 20

The porter returned a little before nine.

"Mr. Kinchloe's party has just come down," he reported. "Table one in the main dining room. As you wished, you have not been announced. *Bon appétit, messieurs.*"

Stanton smiled wryly as he and Tito stepped out the formal entrance of their suite into the thickly carpeted main hall of the residential portion of the building and the lamplight gleaming brightly in reflection from the long double row of ornately paneled walnut doors. *Bon appétit:* good appetite! About as unlikely a salutation as could be had under the circumstances.

No man has an appetite for death, whether his own or that of another. Or even a brush with death, for that matter. Yet at best that was what this would be. There could be no doubt of that.

He swung along silently on his crutches,

acutely conscious of their clumsiness and his own instability upon them. Tito continued to glance at him occasionally in a kind of persisting disbelief but he also remained silent.

At the end of the corridor down which they moved was a short, broad, marble-floored transverse hall which connected the imposing main entrance of the Sans Souci to an elegant bay containing the main desk and forming a small foyer. Across this was a wide flight of three marble steps descending through a richly draped archway into the main dining room.

This room was enormous, easily convertible into a ballroom for hundreds whenever occasion warranted. Like the rest of the establishment it was opulently decorated and furnished and brilliantly lighted by a galaxy of crystal chandeliers. Against the wall on each side was a stairway rising to overhanging balconies connecting with other upper rooms.

At the far end was a small stage from which a considerable runway projected out among the tables to display better the legs of high-kicking girls when entertainment was afforded. A runner of rich, red carpeting stretched from the foot of the marble steps down the center of the room to the runway.

Well-patronized dining tables with spotless linen and gleaming silver were grouped on either side. One table, round and somewhat larger than the others, was placed at the end of the runway at the head of the long strip of red carpeting. This,

Stanton knew, would be table number one.

Before they unwillingly caught the eye of the maître d'hôtel at the foot of the steps, Stanton pulled Tito aside to the shelter of the drapes flanking the archway. Parting the hangings, they had a clear view of the big room without being visible to the diners.

John Kinchloe sat in the host's seat at the big, round table. He was directly facing the entry, perfectly situated for Stanton's purpose. Bucketed champagne was at his elbow and a waiter was pouring freely for his guests. These consisted of two men and three unusually attractive and well-dressed girls whom Stanton guessed to be high-priced members of the professional house staff.

He could make little of the two men except to be reasonably certain at least one wore a gun of some sort beneath the long skirt of his dinner coat. There was considerable banter passing between Kinch's table and others nearby at which were seated several men of obvious wealth and importance with whom he seemed acquainted.

Stanton spoke softly and swiftly to Tito.

"We'll start in together, side by side and unhurried. Head straight for his table, for him. Stay with me until he sees and recognizes us. The instant he does, cut away from me and angle through the tables to the left to a place under that balcony where you can see him and those around him.

"Don't watch Kinch. I'll have my eyes on him.

But keep a sharp lookout for anybody else who looks like they might mix in so you can warn me. If shooting starts and any of it comes your way, hit the floor and dive under a table. Understand?"

Tito nodded. Accusation was again in his eyes but he did not voice it.

"Let's go," Stanton said.

They moved out from the drapes and turned down the marble steps, Stanton very cautious of his crutches on the polished stone. The maître d'hôtel came quickly forward to intercept them. Stanton gestured him aside with a swing of one crutch.

"We're joining friends and prefer to announce ourselves," he said.

The houseman bowed slightly and stepped back. They passed him and moved unhurriedly down the long runner of red carpeting. Half a dozen awkwardly swinging strides. Half a dozen more. Kinchloe was in animated conversation with a girl leaning intimately toward him. Suddenly he saw them and broke off abruptly, stiffening in his seat. The champagne glass beside him overturned unnoticed.

Instantly Tito veered away and angled through the tables on the left. Stanton's eyes did not follow him but remained fixed on Kinchloe. It worked as he had hoped. Kinchloe tried to keep his eyes on both of them at once as they separated, and it distracted him.

"Stanton!" he croaked with the hoarseness of utter disbelief.

He thrust back in his chair and surged to his feet. The man on the other side of the girl to whom Kinchloe had been talking — the guest Stanton thought might be armed — also surged up from the table and cut off through neighboring tables in the same direction Tito had taken. Stanton was sharply alarmed at this but there was no help for it now. He knew what had to be done. There was no other way.

He continued to swing along on his crutches. All sound had ceased in the room. All eyes were on him and Jack Kinchloe. Another swinging stride and Kinchloe called sharply.

"That's far enough, Stanton! Stay where you are."

"We've come for the money you stole from us, Kinchloe," Stanton answered steadily. "Sign it over and we'll go as we came. Don't and I'll have to get close enough to make sure I kill you where you stand."

"Damn you, I said that's far enough! Don't make me do it, Stanton."

Stanton continued to swing rhythmically toward him, his splinted leg hanging clear of the carpeting. Kinchloe waited two more strides before he moved. Then his guns were in his hands, firing at Stanton across the round table before he could free a hand to reach for his own weapon.

But the lead was not meant for his body. Not yet. Not in the open before a hundred stunned onlookers like this. One crutch and then the other was torn from beneath his arms, shattered, and sent skittering across the floor.

Stanton had thought of this, too, and knew what he must do if it happened, whether it cost him his leg or his life. What was started had to be finished. It was the only chance with a man like Kinchloe.

Deprived of the support of his crutches, he did not interrupt his unhurried forward motion. Instead he stepped down firmly on the stirrup iron reinforcing his splint, took his weight upon it, and continued his stride like a one-legged man on a wooden peg.

The iron held and with it the splint and the leg. There was no give in Tito's tightly bound wrappings, no wince of pain, no agony of rebroken bone. Only an uneven gait, far less awkward than that with the crutches, and he had the use of his hands again. Under his breath, he blessed the patient Dutch woodcarver at Manykill and Dr. Jed Magruder.

"The money, Kinchloe," he repeated quietly. "Get much closer and even I can't miss."

"You stubborn bastard," Kinchloe yelled at him furiously. He kicked the big table viciously out of his way, spilling one of the frightened girls from her chair, and started forward with a gun in each hand. "I'll break your damned leg for good, this time!"

One of the guns fired. A tremendous blow smashed Stanton's splinted leg from beneath him. He was spun violently about and went down heavily. As he hit the floor he heard Tito's voice, cracking violently to a high pitch of alarm.

"Spence . . . !"

Stanton rolled over frantically, freeing his own weapon as he did so. Tito was under the left-hand balcony as he had been ordered. Stanton saw that the male guest who had slipped away from Kinchloe's table at the first challenge had not been headed for Tito after all. He had retreated for safety up the stairs to the balcony and now saw a chance to buy chips to his own advantage in his host's game. He was steadying a pocket gun over the railing at Stanton's sprawl on the floor.

It was a snap shot, lying on his side, but with no time for a bettered position. Stanton dropped hammer first and his gun slammed into the heel of his hand in recoil. The ball apparently struck where it counted. The man on the balcony buckled over the rail. His arm dangled limply and his unfired gun dropped from slackened fingers.

Stanton knew Kinchloe was closing rapidly from the table and with his own gun now in hand he was fair enough game in any man's book after the prior warnings he had been given and the warning shots Kinchloe had fired. He scrambled up onto his knees and lunged up onto his good foot and iron-shod splint. Magruder's and the Dutchman's work still held.

As he rose, Stanton saw Tito across the room reach high in a leaping jump and snag in midair the gun dropped by the man on the balcony. As

Kinchloe had taught him, the weapon seemed to land miraculously in Tito's hand, sighted and ready to fire. His voice rang out sharply again.

"Kinch — don't turn!"

Completing his own defensive pivot, Stanton saw Kinchloe caught with one upraised foot where he was halted in midstride. He was rigidly facing Stanton three paces away, his guns before him, every muscle of his body frozen and motionless.

"Drop them, Kinch," Tito's voice called, "or I'll kill you before you can move. You know I can."

Very, very slowly, Kinchloe's frozen fingers loosened. His guns dropped to the red carpeting. He stared at them as though in disbelief. A bluff, hearty man from a nearby table rose and retrieved them, looking at the weapons with a disbelief of his own.

Tito came pushing through the tables quickly to them. Kinchloe raised his head and looked at the boy.

"You'd have done it, wouldn't you?" he asked softly. "What you said. Killed me."

"If I'd had to," Tito agreed.

"Why didn't you anyway? You'd have to figure I'd earned it. You and your pa, both."

Tito hesitated a long moment.

"Because you were a friend once," he said slowly.

"There something to the charges this man's made, Kinchloe?" the big man who had retrieved

Kinchloe's guns asked quietly.

"The money's his," Kinchloe said. "I took it from him when he was laid up with that leg in Leavenworth."

The big man turned to Stanton.

"I'm Ed Farrady, Commercial Bank of St. Louis — Mr. Stanton, is it?" he said. "The money in question's on deposit with us. Most of it anyway. I'll send for proper transfer forms. But since this is a private matter rather than a public one I'd recommend we retire to your rooms. If you're registered here."

Stanton nodded and led the way with Tito. He found he walked awkwardly but easily on his iron-shod splint. He remembered the blow that had felled him and stopped, feeling of his lower leg. There was a bullet tear in the fabric of his pants leg. There was also a deep gouge in the tight outer bindings of the splint, but cloth and wood had turned the ball with no ill effects.

"I'm a son of a bitch!" he murmured, louder than he intended.

Tito smiled in spite of himself. Behind them Kinchloe muttered assent.

"That you sure in hell are, Spence."

"You'll want to press charges, I assume?" the banker asked as they moved down the corridor toward the suite.

"Against Kinch?" Stanton asked. "No." He dropped a hand to Tito's shoulder. "As my partner here said, he was a friend when we needed one. We only want what's ours. I won't

266

take his freedom from him. Or what he's earned. But I'll sure as hell balk at the bonus I promised. Ought to be enough for him to settle up when he clears out of here."

At the door of the suite, Stanton paused.

"What's the stage schedule from here to Santa Fe this season, Mr. Farrady?" he asked.

"Eight — eight and a half days, this time of year."

"Two days off to Willow Springs, plus four hours to the Corona. Any luck, son, we ought to be home for next Sunday dinner. Tell you what, Mr. Farrady, you and Kinchloe figure what's owed and send me over a draft in the morning made out to the Corona Trust and Guaranty Company, Santa Fe, New Mexico, Saul Wetzel, President."

"I know Wetzel, on paper at least. I've done business with him. But I didn't know he had a bank out there."

"He doesn't. That draft's it. But you'll be hearing more of it directly. A lot more. Now if you'll excuse us, Tito and I have to pack."

Kinchloe hung back for a moment to say something, but in the end he could not find the words and left with the banker in silence. When they had entered the suite and closed the door behind them, Spencer Stanton fixed a firm eye on his son.

"You've gotten so you handle a gun tolerably well when there's a need, but you still got to watch your language some," he said.

Tito blinked curiously.

"What did I say wrong now?"

"Not what you said. What you called me when you thought that bastard on the balcony was going to put a bullet into my back."

"I was sure scared he would. Spence . . . did I call you Spence?"

"You did. And I don't know as I mind at all. I never did think too much of Pa. But it's sure going to take your mother a spell to get used to. That and that gun in your belt. I'll never make you take it off again."

The employees of G.K. Hall hope you have enjoyed this Large Print book. All our Large Print titles are designed for easy reading, and all our books are made to last. Other G.K. Hall books are available at your library, through selected bookstores, or directly from us.

For information about titles, please call:

(800) 223-1244
(800) 223-6121

To share your comments, please write:

Publisher
G.K. Hall & Co.
P.O. Box 159
Thorndike, ME 04986